MW01712371

Praise for the Tales of the Captain Duke

"…just when things seem to start coming together, Diem drops one of the most shocking cliff hangers I've had to deal with in a while. And now I am impatiently awaiting the next book!"

– Wendy (BiblioSanctum)

"Excellent pacing and the intrigue has built to a wicked tipping point! I can't wait to see what happens next!"

– Jamie Sigal (Goodreads)

"An emotional roller-coaster ride of quick decisions, battles, friendships and enemies. Never certain who do you trust and the unobvious outcome always a heart beating, breathless surprise. Fall in love again. Align your heart with one of the characters in this book and be prepared...things aren't always as they appear."

– Robert Thistle (Goodreads)

"Oh my! What a fantastic story! I loved every moment of the series. Difficult to put down!"

– Amanda Chamberlain (Goodreads)

"This has been a hard series to put down…Rebecca is an up and coming writer to follow in the future and I look forward to checking out her future projects."

– Sam (Tattered Turtle's Tittle Tattle)

Also by Rebecca Diem:

Tales of the Captain Duke

The Stowaway Debutante

From Haven to Hell

A Gentleman and a Scholar

Of Tempests and Teacups

Tales of the Captain Duke

Of Tempests and Teacups

Rebecca Diem

Eliana, to new horizons! R. Diem

WOOLF LIKE ME
Publishing
R, D

Cover art by Sarah Dier-McComb
Cover design by Steve Armstrong

First Edition

Woolf Like Me Publishing
ISBN: 978-1-7752719-0-1

This book is dedicated to you, my crew.
Thank you for being on this adventure with me!

Table of Contents

Chapter 1: In which our heroine takes the helm

Cat was watching when the man she was following made a grave error. Every day for the past week he had followed the same route. Down the street, across the crowded square, past the chapel and into the market. Always surrounded, always protected by the hustle and bustle of London. But today, he acted oddly, ducking into shops and taking sudden turns onto side streets, all while casting furtive glances over his shoulder.

She watched as he entered the old church. And she watched as two more shadows slipped in behind him. Cat was not the only one marking his steps.

The building was as high as a tallport, with grand masonry depicting images of saints whose names and faces had long been weathered away. The stone was smooth, but moss had grown into the cracks, and Cat had an easy enough time climbing up to an open window where linens were hung to dry in the crisp autumn air. She listened to make sure the room was empty after tossing a small pebble inside. She was careful not to disturb the stockings and collar hanging around the sill as she entered the modest living quarters. Slipping down a stairwell and into the vestibule, she caught sight of her quarry once more through the decorative slats of the choir stalls.

The old butler was seated on one of the long, wooden

benches, his head bowed in prayer. When he looked up, the unhappy lines on his face had settled into tranquil contemplation.

"I would know the reason I am being followed, if you please."

Cat froze. How could he have detected her? She remained absolutely still until a man moved out of a shadowy alcove on the opposite side of the hall. The others, of course. She stifled her sigh of relief.

"You have an astute eye, Mr. Tores. We mean you no harm. My colleague and I merely hoped to catch a glimpse of your employer."

"As I have repeatedly stated, Master Olivier is missing."

"And this is unusual? Why, I understand he travels quite frequently, does he not?"

He held his tongue as the henchmen approached. One man took up a position at the far end of the pew, taciturn and silent with a heavyset frame. His companion was bolder. He strolled down the centre aisle and lifted a muddy boot to scrape the dead leaves off on the iron lattice of the arm rest. Then he entered the row in front of the butler to lean casually against the rail.

"Listen, Sebastian—may I call you Sebastian? I'm not inclined to violence in the house of the Lord, but my friend here ain't so saintly as I."

"I've made my peace. I have nothing to say to you."

"Stubborn old man. I'm trying to help you. Tell me, what was the last you saw of him?"

"I spoke to the constable, you may confer with him at your leisure."

"And what of the others who visited you? The women? Were you more forthcoming with them?"

Silence.

"If you will not speak of your master, will you tell me of them?"

"You leave those gentlewomen alone, you hear me?"

Cat gave a wry grin. She was certain Nessa would appreciate the servant's efforts to defend them, ineffective as they were before such brutal curs as these. The speaker was laughing, his dark overcoat billowing as his shoulders shook with affected mirth. He raised his face enough for her to see it beneath the brim of his hat. A younger man than she might have expected, with dark brown hair and a carefully waxed moustache. Cat remained hidden, slipping her throwing knives from the secret pocket in her boot.

"Listen, Sebastian, what if I told you that I, too, am quite invested in discovering the whereabouts of your master? In fact, I would pay dearly for any information."

"Even if I knew, I'd never tell the likes of you!"

Cat was startled by the suddenness of the blow that followed. The violent turn lasted but a moment, so quick that she might have doubted its occurrence had the victim not crumpled to the bench, senseless. The man at the centre aisle regarded his victim with an air of impassiveness that sent a chill down her spine.

"Mr. Corring, sir, I don't think—," the other man began to speak.

"You are not meant to think. Leave that to your betters," he replied.

"But the Admiral said we were to follow 'im. Bring 'im in to say if it were his master we snatched. He's been making a lot of noise about Olivier going missing. Folks might think he's got the right of it if they find 'im like this."

The man called Corring frowned, "He wouldn't have told us anything. Besides, I know it's him. It must be. Damn the Admiral! Olivier, the Captain Duke—I don't care one whit about who he is. We should kill him and be done with it."

He turned and began to walk to the doors.

"Sir? What about the butler?"

"Search him," he called over his shoulder. "Make it look like a robbery gone awry if you like. It matters not. We'll be away by the time he's got the sense to tell anyone."

Finding nought but a small purse of coins, the henchman hurried to exit the old church.

Cat waited as long as she dared before dashing across the room in a low crouch to check on the old butler, using the pews as cover. She placed two fingers at his pulse while checking the goose egg on his forehead. Still breathing, still alive, though likely to be rather sore upon awakening. She made sure he was comfortable before retracing her steps. But as she rounded a corner, her vision was filled by a set of heavy black robes.

"You, child, what are you doing in here?"

Cat's breath caught for but a moment, before she looked to the portly clergyman with feigned alarm.

"Oh, sir! I was searching for you. There is a man who requires your assistance in the vestibule. I believe he has struck his head and sustained an injury."

"Ah, I will attend to him presently."

Cat did her best to summon tears to underscore the necessity of an immediate response. Her efforts were futile, but the priest nonetheless hurried past her to look after his new charge. She took a breath and relaxed her grip on the throwing knife still concealed in her sleeve. Tucking it back into her boot, she slipped into the room he had vacated and onto the sill before climbing higher, scaling the walls until she could follow the peaked roof to the front of the cathedral. The two had hidden themselves, poorly, in the churchyard. Likely watching for someone to come to the old butler's aid.

Tempting as it was to follow them, orders were orders and Cat had strict instructions not to engage. There could be others, and she had what she came for anyways. She made her way to the back of the roof, taking the glider from the satchel across her back and harnessing herself into its straps. Expanding the wings, she checked the breeze before leaping into the air and banking sharply to catch the draft that would carry her due west, out of sight of the market square and the men who waited there.

Soaring over the squalid streets of London, she wrinkled her nose. The sooner they could leave for the open skies the better. She longed for an end to this intrigue the way she longed for the fresh scent of the lake district. And the ever-present anxiety curled in the pit of her stomach at being separated from her brother for so long, despite the regular missives from Trick and Archie at Lovelace University reassuring her that all was well.

The docklands came into view, with its soaring tallports filled with airships from every latitude and longitude of the known world. Cat practiced a flip before landing lightly on the deck of the airship, her glider wings tucked in a perfect fold across her back. She nodded to the lookout before making her way straight for the Captain's quarters. After three sharp knocks, she entered, closing the door firmly behind her.

"Cat, you've returned early today. What news?"

The blue coat was hung on a hook by the door. The bed in the room beyond was neatly made. Maps and missives covered the large desk at the centre of the room. Clara rose from the chair behind it and crossed her arms.

Chapter 2: In which our heroine finds past and present intertwined

Clara was not feeling particularly charitable that day. It was peak season for the transport of this year's harvest and she had spent the morning pouring over reports from the pirate crews spread across the British Isles. Her plan to divide the crew into smaller parties led by regional officers had been met with great success. They had even recruited more pilots to their cause, tithing the ships of the Association of Merchant Traders—the Tradists, as they were commonly known—as inspectors. The indomitable Peg and her company had the north. Madge, along with her ever-present bag of clever tricks and potions, took the Midlands and Wales. Himmat Singh and his aircrew covered the many trade lines of the southwest, with Nessa keeping their London operations in check. But as they grew in number, so too did the risk of discovery.

They funnelled the illicit goods into a black market run by Master Tims. His alliance of charitable vendors and shopkeepers used the additional stock to counter the extortionist rates charged by the Tradists, who had few friends among the general populace thanks to their brutal treatment of local retailers and any who threatened their monopoly. The Captain Duke and his first mate, Trick Killarney, had formed their enterprise to fight back, staying one step ahead of the Tradists and putting goods back in the hands of honest folk.

Lately, it seemed, their luck had run out.

The Haven, the pirate's refuge, was lost. Half-burnt and compromised thanks to the traitorous Robbie and a clandestine shipment of gunpowder. The crews were to regroup before the storm season began. They needed new quarters, but Clara barely had time to consider that particular hindrance amid the problems they faced. The mystery of the gunpowder weighed on her mind—where had it come from and why were the Tradists so concerned with getting it back? It seemed to be at the centre of all their troubles. It was difficult to believe that only months ago she had come across the illicit cargo while stowing away on an airship, eager to leave her life as a debutante behind her, wanting to carve her own path through the skies.

The destruction of the Haven had led to their dispersion. Now, Clara feared that the disappearance of the Captain Duke might leave them scattered.

Clara felt untethered. Had he been kidnapped? Killed? They had checked every one of their sources in London, made discreet inquiries to the mechanicab dispatcher, the tallportmaster, the butler. There had been no sighting of him since the evening of Mrs. Branson-Honeycutt's salon—the night Clara had spent in his bedchamber, alone.

Barely a month ago he had named her quartermaster. And now, she was the acting captain. She had tried to convince Nessa or Trick to take charge, to no avail. A technicality—as quartermaster, she was next in rank.

And here was little Cat, her teacher and confidante, attempting seriousness as she relayed the morning's misadventures.

"I followed the butler, as you asked, Quartermaster.

Your suspicions were correct, he was followed. They tried to intimidate him, but he kept our confidences."

Clara sighed, "I hope Sebastian was not badly hurt. I truly did not think he held us in such high regard, but his loyalty to the Captain Duke—or rather, to Olivier, remains steadfast. But you saw them? Did they see you?"

"No, I stayed out of sight. And I wasn't followed. I took the long way 'round just in case. They struck him, but he'll survive. It did more to loosen their tongues than his."

Clara had begun to tidy the accounting ledgers and receipt books stacked on the desk, filing them by region and by date on shelves built into the corner of the room. As Cat spoke, she froze. Every muscle tensed as she waited for the answer to a question she dared not give voice.

"I overheard them speaking," Cat continued. "The Captain is alive. For now, at least."

Letting out a breath she did not know she had been holding, Clara turned and sank heavily into the chair, gesturing for Cat to sit as well.

"Tell me what we know."

"There were two of them. They said the Admiral is protecting him for some reason."

"Admiral Flint?"

"They didn't say, but I suspect so. They were tasked with getting the butler to confirm if they had the right man. They failed in that regard. But the one didn't seem so concerned about his identity."

Cat paused, fidgeting with her hem.

Clara raised an eyebrow, "And?"

"I heard the one call the other by the name Corring. Dark hair, moustache, wears his arrogance like a second skin."

"Alexander," Clara said, narrowing her eyes. "Alexander Corring has the Captain?"

The chair clattered to the floor as she stood, crossing the room to open the door, Cat close on her heels. She had fled the Isle of Wight after learning the true character of her betrothed. Corring had plagued her ever since, refusing to acknowledge their broken engagement. He had threatened her family. He had threatened her crew. And now, he had the life of her Captain in his treacherous hands.

Alive. The Captain Duke is alive.

She repeated the refrain to herself, a mantra of calm in a tempest as her thoughts tumbled together. The night of the salon. Dancing in his arms, all whispers and smiles. Their last conversation before he vanished. The pirate captain, the gentleman scholar – one and the same. Free to roam the skies as the legendary Captain Duke, and to return to London for the storm seasons under his christened name, Marmaduke Ivan Lysander Olivier. Milo. Clara had only made the discovery herself the week prior to the salon. In fairness, she too had kept her true name a secret when she talked her way into joining his crew.

Clara and Cat made their way to the aft deck. Seeing them hurrying towards her, Nessa dismissed the crew members she had been speaking with to their duties.

"What news? Has there been word?"

"He's alive. And we know who has him," Clara replied.

Nessa's eyes grew wide as Cat repeated her report on the morning's activities. The young pilot had taken on a greater role in their strategy sessions of late. She was indispensable in organizing the movement of the crews and keeping records of the bounty they brought in. And it was thanks to her eavesdropping the night of the salon that they had information on the intentions of the Tradist faction led by Admiral Flint—and his connection to Professor Sewell and her work with Clara's brother at the university in Reading.

Cat finished her account, "I would have followed them, but…"

"No. No, you did the right thing," said Nessa. "We have other means of discovering his location, now that we know Flint and Corring are involved in his abduction."

"They think they have the gentleman and not the pirate, not realising they are one and the same. We should encourage their confusion," Clara mused. "It could keep him safe."

"Or he could lose his value as a hostage," said Nessa. "Do you think they will simply let him leave on a case of mistaken identity? You cannot place your trust in good intentions."

"Ness is right," said Cat, looking between them. "They attacked a man in a church. These are ruthless types. We should be careful."

"Careful, but clever," said Clara. "Corring suspects. But it is the Admiral's confidence we must concern ourselves with. If we can encourage the division between them..."

"I like your thinking. But how?" asked Nessa.

"I have an idea, but we'll need assistance. And we'll need the Professor."

Cat raised an eyebrow, "You trust her? Still?"

Professor Georgina Jameson Sewell was a genius inventor, head of Lovelace University's biomechanical engineering department and a close friend and colleague of Clara's brother, Archie Whittington. The evening of the salon, Cat had discovered the Professor slipping away to meet with the Admiral Flint and his allies. While her work with Archie focused on prosthetics, helping those affected by injury or illness, the Tradists were interested in the militaristic applications of her research. The exact nature of their agreement was unknown—they knew that she had shown the Tradists drawings of a mechanical soldier prototype, spoke of a demonstration of some kind—but soon after the meeting, Professor Sewell had received a coveted invitation to mount an exhibition at London's Crystal Palace, showcasing her work and the work of Lovelace's students.

Clara shook her head, "Trust? No. But she has value if we wish to get closer to the Admiral."

"And if she catches on?" asked Cat. "If she sides with the Tradists against us, she could betray us."

"The Professor suspects nothing. She believes that our extended stay in London is to visit friends. She actually heaped praises on Marie in her last letter and invited us all for tea at Lovelace if you're ever travelling over Reading."

"That could be a front," Nessa said, shaking her head. "Tea parties and toy soldiers. She's an unusual sort."

"I am not suggesting we confide in her. But something about this strikes me as odd. I cannot say what, except—she has helped so many. She helped Trick—not just with his physical rehabilitation, she helped bring back his music as well. I believe in her heart she is on our side. But sometimes good people are compromised by complicated factors. I would like to know what those factors are."

Cat nodded, "Very well, but we need to act quickly. Corring mentioned they were preparing to move the Captain."

"And the Lovelace showcase is next week," Nessa said, crossing her arms. "We need to find out what the Professor and the Tradists are up to, and soon."

Clara felt the anxious stirrings in her chest but did her best to maintain an outward air of assurance. They needed more evidence of her connection to Admiral Flint and the Tradists, and her intentions for the prototype she planned to display. Archie's obvious affection for Professor Sewell was a complication. They had decided to keep her brother in the dark, to lessen the risk of alarming the Professor or the Tradists before they were ready to act. Clara was not looking forward to casting aspersions on the woman he held in such high esteem. For now, she was content to have him believe the only source of her worries was the Captain's disappearance.

"We'll stop the Tradists and save the Captain Duke. That's our plan. Cat, send a message to Trick and Mouse in Reading. Tell them we need more information on the Professor's prototype. They'll be coming to prepare for the showcase soon. We can all assemble here in London," Clara said, before turning to Nessa. "Meanwhile, we can track down Thompson at the inn, see what he has to say now that we know the Admiral and Corring are involved."

Cat gave a firm nod and ran off to compose a message

for the wireless, using the codex she and Mouse had developed to encrypt their dispatches to the crews. Nessa placed a hand on Clara's arm before leaving to gather her things and give instructions to the crew.

Clara wanted to feel reassured but instead she was wracked with guilt. What if they had misplaced their trust in her abilities? What if she failed them all?

Chapter 3: In which our hero is entangled in a turn of fortune

The Captain Duke lay on the narrow bed, watching the small panel of light mark its path across the wall. It was half past the unfortunate stain, nearing the bent nail that stuck out at an odd angle—which meant his captors should have brought his dinner by now.

The boredom of captivity would have been bad enough. Not to mention the throbbing of his head for the first days of his recovery. But it was the fear that drove him mad. Was Clara safe? Had she been taken too? Did his crew even know he was missing?

The walls were thin, and the Captain Duke was using every opportunity to learn more of his assailants. The young one with the big ears was a recent conscript, who'd looked to join a war but missed his opportunity to prove himself. The burly one with the beard textured like a chimney brush was the least talkative but had the heaviest step. The third was absolutely unremarkable, with dour eyes and mousy brown hair. Terrible inconvenience for his chosen profession, as one could hardly be a proper henchman without some sort of distinguishing characteristic. Their leader, as far as he could tell, was an arrogant popinjay who spent too much time before the mirror with his moustache.

His only comfort was the apparent success of Clara's scheme. With the crews scattered to the four winds posing as inspectors, there had been no reported pirate attacks in months on the common merchant trading vessels or heavy transports. The soldiers employed by the Tradists to protect the ships had suffered lost wages and a fair share of frustration from the sound of it.

Of course, he had to pretend to know nothing of the sort, to continue his ruse as a gentleman scholar. Here, the Captain Duke had the advantage. For years he'd curated his dual identities, the double life he had led since inheriting his mother's estate. As Marmaduke Olivier, his credentials were flawless. An orphaned son of a tradesman, born of an illicit affair with a duchess and secreted away at birth to be raised by his father. He was named the sole heir to the Olivier estate after his mother 'adopted' him on her deathbed, and set off to become an explorer.

Not for the last time did he thank his stars that he had been taken by them not in the garb of a pirate, but of a gentleman of finer class. Though his clothes had become somewhat rank in the intervening weeks of his captivity, he had survived worse in the past. And he had his answers at the ready for their interrogations, feigning ignorance of their motives in his capture though they tried their best to prove he was the pirate captain they sought. As soon as he woke, he demanded they release him, giving his full name and the address of his London home. He hoped their confusion might be enough to extricate himself from this predicament—or at the least, buy him enough time to plan an escape.

Boots on the back stairs. Someone who did not wish to be seen.

He sat up, the heavy chains clanking gently between his ankles. He stood and stretched before returning to sit on the bed. Posture straight, shackled wrists resting on his parted knees. A posture of calm masking coiled tension as he prepared for whatever—or whoever—waited beyond the locked door.

Chapter 4: In which our heroine fails to see a silver lining

Clara ignored the curious stares as she walked with Nessa along the streets of London. Clara had chosen her grey dress, the one she had used in the inspector scheme, with split seams sewn by the clever Mrs. Cottingham for access to the weapons concealed in her skirts. Nessa wore slim trousers tucked into tall boots and a pale blue jacket with two rows of brass buttons, tapered at the waist before flaring slightly over her hips. Thanks to the rational dress movement, it was less rare to see a woman in trousers beyond the docklands and airbours, but the cyclists in their bloomers did not command attention as Nessa did. She walked with the air of a woman not to be trifled with, shoulders back and head held high. Her long, blonde braid was fastened with a gleaming azure cuff—a gift from her beloved, Marie Buchanan.

Captain of a fleet of airships that traversed the globe, Marie was the greatest pilot to ever fly the Atlantic trade winds. Her business relied on good relations with the Tradists, but she had proven to be an ally of the Captain Duke and his allies throughout their long acquaintance.

"What is it?" Nessa asked Clara, catching her gaze.

Clara grinned, "You're dressed exceptionally fine today. Should we expect you for dinner with the crew tonight?"

"I have an invitation to join Marie this evening," Nessa said, colour rising in her cheeks. "But perhaps I should send word to her, to cancel our plans."

"Nonsense, I see no need to spoil your evening. We will make our attempt to find this Thompson and return in due time," Clara said. Then she gave a sidelong glance at her friend, "Has there been any progress in her negotiations with the Tradists?"

Nessa rolled her eyes. "No. In fact, she's sent *Fregata* on to the Caribbean without her and rented a house in Chelsea for the storm season."

Clara raised a brow, "Did they think she would yield to them if they delayed, and leave to beat the storms?"

Nessa flicked her braid over her shoulder in irritation.

"I'm certain that was the plan. Their current agreement was struck when she was newly widowed and the target of a campaign of harassment by her husband's awful family. Now, they need her as much as she needs them. None of the other trading vessels can hold a candle to her fleet. Her deckhands can outfly their best captains in a storm. Her loss rate is negligible compared to theirs, and yet she pays a higher commission on every cargo. It's not fair. She plans to fight them until they grant her more favourable terms, and she's settling in for a long fight."

"Dreadful. Tell Marie she has our support, if there is anything we can do."

"She'll be pleased to hear it. Ah, here we are."

The pub was nondescript, with a faded wooden sign hanging above the door declaring itself as The Tinker's Tavern. Its patrons were of moderate means, tradespersons and travellers mostly. Nessa scanned the tables and booths before heading for a seat near the innkeeper, busy polishing the bar.

"Has a man by the name of Thompson been here of late?"

Thompson had captained the airship carrying the gunpowder—and Clara—from the Isle of Wight, bound for London when it was intercepted by the Captain Duke and his crew. The traitorous former officer Robbie had brokered a deal with Thompson in exchange for his life, but Robbie's plotting to return the gunpowder to Corring had ended in a failed mutiny. Nessa and the Captain Duke had discovered Thompson in London, rather worse for wear after disappointing his Tradist connections—he had quaked with fear while giving them the name of Admiral Flint. They had checked the tavern after the Captain's disappearance to no avail. But now that they knew of Corring's involvement, Clara was determined to retrace every lead.

The innkeeper ducked behind the bar to pull out a sealed envelope, offering it to Nessa. She raised an eyebrow, then dropped a few coins on the bar for his trouble.

"What does it say?" Clara asked, as Nessa broke the seal and skimmed the contents.

Something fell as she unfolded the note within, and Clara caught it by instinct: a lock of fiery red hair. Her heart stilled as she stared at the strands, knotted together in the palm of her hand. Nessa covered it with her own hand, forcing Clara to meet her eyes.

"It's an address. Not far from here," she said, before turning back to the innkeeper. "How long ago did he leave this?"

"Haven't seen Thompson for a fortnight at least. He settled his tab and scampered. It was a friend of his who dropped it off, maybe three, four days ago? Said to give it to any lasses coming in asking for Thompson. Why? What's the trouble?"

"Thank you," Clara spoke. "You see, the damnable cur tried to seduce my niece, but it seems he's skipped town. Do keep an eye out for him, will you?"

Indignant, the innkeeper swore he would send word if Thompson showed his face again. They wove their way through the streets and lanes, ducking into shops and turning back on their steps and hovering in alleys until they were certain they were not being followed. Nessa led the way, circling back to a small glove shop. The bell chimed as they entered, but Nessa ignored the contents of the shop, hovering near the front window with a view of the street.

"It's there," she said, indicating an alley across the way.

"They cut his hair," Clara said, her voice unsteady. "Ness—,"

"I know. But think, Clara. We had word he's alive as early as this morning. This note was left days ago."

"But why?"

"To draw us out, perhaps. This is where the Captain saw them meeting. We followed Robbie's contact to this place. Saw him with Thompson the day we confronted him. Hells. I should have put an end to this that day."

"They must be holding him here. Nessa, we have to help him."

"And how do you propose we do that? Walk up to the

door and knock?"

"Cat said they planned to move him, what if we're too late? We must act now."

"Good afternoon, ladies. May I assist you?"

They turned. The young woman in charge of the shop was standing there expectantly.

"Oh, you're back," her smile brightened as she saw Nessa. "Have you come for gloves?"

"Why, yes. Something practical this time, leather or somesuch if you have any in the back," said Nessa, before turning back to the window.

The woman crossed her arms, "If you're looking for your friend, you've just missed him. They already left."

Clara and Nessa traded a look.

"I beg your pardon," Clara began. "Who did?"

"The gentleman with the red hair and his companions." She chatted happily as she buzzed around the shop, making minute adjustments to the immaculate display, "Business can be slow sometimes, so I entertain myself by observing the activity of the general populace."

"Please, tell us what you know," said Clara. "It's very important that we find him."

"Are you even interested in the gloves?" the woman asked, frowning.

Nessa gave her a shrewd look, "We'll take two pairs."

The glovemaker pulled a measuring tape from the

pocket of her apron and began measuring Nessa's wrist.

"Well, I think there may be some kind of gentleman's lounge across the way, or a secret clubhouse. The man you came in with the other day was pulled out by his friends, perhaps an hour ago. Looked rather worse for wear, I do say, as though he'd been drinking all night. Nearly knocked his friend over and tried to run away while they were getting him into the mechanicab—it took all four of them in the end. I'm sure he's already on his way home to sleep off the effects of the evening's merriment."

Clara's face fell. They had been so close—and now they were practically back where they started, with no idea of where he was being held. She felt a sense of panic rising and did her best to quell it as Nessa gave a nearly imperceptible shake of her head.

"Well… there you have it," said Nessa. "Clara, we should be on our way. We probably passed them on the street. They'll be nearly home by now."

"Yes, thank you," said Clara.

"No trouble," the woman smiled. "Shall I wrap your gloves, or would you care to wear them now?"

Hands encased in supple leather, they made their way back to the east docklands in silence. Clara's distress grew with each step as thoughts of what could have been raced through her mind. If only they had worked harder to track down Thompson, if only they had discovered the note earlier, if only they had left together the night of the salon…

"Stop it," Nessa spoke at last, pulling her to a halt in an alley as they neared the tallport.

"What is it?" Clara asked, scanning their surroundings. "Are we being followed?"

"I've seen no one. But you must stop tormenting yourself and focus on what's before you. We could have walked right past the Captain and you would not have noticed, lost in your thoughts as such."

"This is all my fault," Clara whispered, feeling the prick of tears as she finally spoke the words aloud. She searched her friend's face for the judgement she was certain she deserved. "All of it."

Nessa clasped her hands in her own, the brown leather of Clara's gloves interlocked with her camel ones.

"No, Clara. You are not responsible for the actions of cowardly men. Thompson must have fled the city, which means they're likely seeking someone else to confirm the Captain's identity. The innkeeper said so himself: someone else left the note. The letter was bait. Even if we had rushed in to rescue him, they would have expected us, and they would have their proof he is more than the scholarly Olivier," she said, before reaching out to put an arm over Clara's shoulder. "We know that he is alive, and that he is being held by Alexander Corring and at least three others. That's better than yesterday."

"If I had never run away, Alexander would have no reason to threaten the Captain's life."

"If you had never run away, you might be wed to that dreadful man, and the Tradists' scheming would go unchecked," Nessa reminded.

Clara let out a laugh that was half-sob, half-hiccough. There were worse choices she could have made than running away that day. It felt as though an age had passed since that day in July, but the calendar was just now creeping towards November. Four months and a lifetime ago.

"What do we do now?" Clara asked.

Chapter 5: In which our heroine charts a new course

That evening, as the electric lamps flickered to life and twilight gave way to dusk, Clara glided over the jewel-lit streets, seeking a clear mind. The fog swirled with the eddies of the water as she followed the Thames, swooping around the construction at the new crossing by the Tower.

Her crew was divided and on the run from an enemy with more power and resources than she had imagined. But Clara had another problem, one she had only recently discovered.

Clara was in love.

She had woken early the morning after the salon to an empty room, still wearing the beautiful lilac ballgown, now crumpled and rather worse for wear. Puzzled by the Captain's absence, and somewhat bashful at the memory of her proposition the evening before, she had slipped out of the cabin and crossed the deck to her own quarters. All was quiet on the airship as dawn broke over the horizon.

Changing into a fresh set of slim trousers and a loose shirt, she had belted a long, embroidered coat gingerly around her waist where the corset had dug angry red lines into her skin as she slept. Her hair still in carefully-wrought ringlets, she had removed the pins one by one until her brown curls fell wild and loose around her face and shoulders. Staring into the small, polished mirror that hung on the wall, Clara had hardly recognized herself—caught in transition between the apportioned halves of her life: part lady, part pirate.

It originated as a sharp pang of fear when she and the others had discovered the Captain Duke was nowhere to be found. Now it manifested as a dull ache in the chambers of her heart. A sense of absence—of his voice, of his touch, even the manner in which he walked into a room. She felt all the acute unfairness of losing him just as she discovered the true nature of her feelings for him. Unspoken words hovered at the tip of her tongue. The cosmos was not so cruel as to part them forever just as she made this discovery. They were meant to explore the world together.

One way or another, she would find her Captain again.

So close, she chided herself, tamping down at the fears that threatened to overwhelm her. They had been so close to finding him today. What if they had missed their only chance?

She longed for his advice. Her time with the pirates had shown her she was capable of so much more than her previous life allowed. This new role, leading hundreds in a campaign to stop the largest trading association in the Empire, plagued her with doubts. Worries that her lack of worldly experience might render her unfit. Worries that pluck and cleverness might fail her in the end. Worries that each and every decision she made might be the wrong one at the wrong time. Worries of the casualties that could follow.

If the Captain Duke were here, he would know exactly what to do.

Or he'd take her hand, pretend to brush a lock of hair aside as an excuse to cup her face, and he'd look her in the eyes as he…

Clara blinked.

Those thoughts were not conducive to clear-headedness.

Of course, if she could not call on her Captain for advice, a visit to another esteemed captain might help her situation. Clara banked her glider's wings and turned herself round towards Chelsea, flying over the fog that encased the city in cloud.

The hour was late when she knocked at the address Nessa had given. A housekeeper answered the door and bade her wait in the entry hall as she hurried off to announce her. Moments later, she returned with one of the *Ariadne's* pilots to collect Clara's outerwear and glider before ushering her upstairs to Captain Buchanan's private quarters.

Clara heard soft voices on the other side of the door as the pilot knocked and announced her.

"Welcome, Clara. To what do we owe this pleasure?" called Captain Marie Buchanan.

Sitting at a mirrored table, the legendary pilot wore an embroidered dressing gown fastened at the waist. Nessa stood at her back, rubbing sweet-smelling oil into her long, dark locs. It was an intimate moment; the two women seemed at home in each other's presence, taking joy in these little domestic activities before the winds of fate parted them once more.

"My apologies, I did not mean to intrude," Clara replied, ducking her head in respect.

"Nonsense, you are always welcome here. Has something happened?"

Clara felt foolish to have interrupted their quiet evening only to air her concerns. But Marie called for brandy and compelled Clara to join them for a nightcap. Soon, she was pouring out all her hopes and fears.

"I just—I cannot shake this feeling that I am a pretender, that somehow I have tricked my way into this role and deluded everyone, myself most of all, into thinking I am capable," Clara said, standing to pace the room. "They all look to me for guidance, and there are times when I truly do not know the answer. In so many ways, I feel I am a silly debutante who's flown too high. I have never felt so lost."

"Clara, do you doubt the trust of your crew?" asked Captain Buchanan.

Nessa made a small noise of protest but was silenced.

Clara sniffed, "No, of course not. But they follow me because the Captain named me quartermaster—it's just a technicality, an arrangement he could not have foreseen."

"Ah, I see the trouble," Marie said, a smile quirking at the side of her lips as she cast a sidelong glance at Nessa. "Clara, the Captain Duke did not name you his successor."

Clara frowned, "What? But Nessa said—"

"That you were next in command, yes. But a pirate captain does not choose his quartermaster, no more than he or she could name themselves captain. That privilege lies with the crew."

As the meaning behind Marie's words sunk in, Clara's mouth opened in astonishment.

"It's true," said Nessa. "I should have remembered that you would not be familiar with our ways. Your name was put forward and the vote was unanimous. That is why the Captain Duke named you."

"But why?"

"Well, you've done nothing but save our lives since the moment we laid eyes on you. You worked like the devil to prove your place among us, trained hard, fought at our sides and outsmarted our enemies. It was your plan to tithe the Tradist ships while hiding in plain sight – masquerading as inspectors, receipt books and all," explained Nessa. "And look at the success we have seen! Master Tims can hardly keep pace with the bounty we acquired this last month alone, and with hardly any harm to our crew. Not as much fighting to be had, sure. But no lives lost either."

Clara felt as though her heart had become caught in her throat. No lives lost since the battle at the Haven. None since Anderssen had died in her arms, his life stolen by Robbie's mutineers. She sat on a low bench, gripping the edge of the seat as the wave of grief broke over her, and took a deep breath.

"So this means…"

"This means that we trust you. We believe in you. A pirate quartermaster leads the raiding parties, acts as a counterbalance to the captain, and can veto his decisions if they're not in the best interests of the crew," said Nessa, coming to sit at her side. "Whatever you decide, we will follow."

"And what if I make the wrong choice?"

"Well, that's why you have Trick and I, to tell you when you're being daft."

"Clara, do you know why Olivier and I became friends?" Marie asked, rising to stand before her. "Not merely allies, but friends? It is because, while we toy with acceptability and the privileges of our class, we never forget where we come from.

"Once upon a time, before his inheritance, before he became the Captain Duke, Olivier was an orphan left to make his own way in the world. I am daughter to a noblewoman and the granddaughter of slaves. We can move in respectable circles, but we know this privilege granted to us could just as easily be taken away. Always, at the foremost of our minds, is who we are fighting for.

"But you, you could set all this behind you, if you wished, and your social class would welcome you back. There would be no lack of scandal, to be sure—the gossips would have no business otherwise. But a woman's place is changing. It is quite acceptable now for a lady to have a taste for adventure and some youthful follies to her name. You have options. Your crew? The merchants? They would starve.

"Your crew has honoured you with this responsibility. They chose you. They believe in you. And now you can walk between worlds. You can use your station to amplify the voices of others. You can find ways to lift up your neighbours and friends. But you must never forget who put you there. Your crew. Your cleverness. And yes, your Captain Duke."

Captain Buchanan's words struck her like a thunderclap. Perceptive, diplomatic, generous—she could understand why her friend was so enamoured with the woman. Nessa looked at Captain Buchanan with such love in her eyes, Clara swore the room grew brighter. She was silent for a long moment, taking in Marie's advice. And she realized what she needed to do.

"Thank you, Marie. And you, Nessa. But I have yet another favour to ask."

Marie gave a slow smile at Clara's look of determination. "I'm listening."

"How do you feel about throwing a dinner party?"

Chapter 6: In which our heroine questions alliances and celebrates old friends

Clara stood at the top of the tallport with Cat at her side, high above the eastern docklands of London. So much had happened in their brief time in the city, she struggled to remember it had been but a few short weeks since they left Reading. Her heart rose at the sight of a blue and purple airship headed their way.

Three figures waved from the helm of the *Flutterby Hum*. Mouse was practically bouncing as he waited for Archie to secure the gangway. And Trick looked younger by a decade, lively and laughing as he held Mouse back with his good hand on the boy's shoulder. As soon as the airship was secure, Mouse bounded across to his sister, wrapping her in a hug.

"Cat! I got to make an autobauble all by myself—with Archie's help—and the Professor let me come to her lectures and said I could go to any that I wanted, so I did and I'm learning chemistry and stuff, just like Madge! But my favourite is physics, and wait 'til you see the book I got!"

Cat pulled her little brother into an embrace and shut her eyes. Clara wisely pretended not to notice the tear that escaped before the young woman wiped it away.

"I see we were not missed at all," Clara said, with a wink to her own brother. She pulled Archie in for a quick embrace before turning to her friend. "Trick, you look well."

"I feel like a new man!" He patted his new arm. A harness was strapped across his chest, fastened with brass trimmings that complemented his new green jacket. At the end of the appendage, however…

"A hook?" Clara asked.

"It amuses me," Trick replied with a wave. "Archie and Mouse crafted a whole suite of accessories. The bow is my favourite, of course. And I have a proper hand for formal occasions, a quill for writing—I think you'll find I have been quite at their mercy."

"The hook was your idea," Archie protested. "And the blade."

Trick glowered, "Shush, that one was meant to be a surprise."

Clara raised an eyebrow, "You have been busy."

"I hope to finish a few more prototypes soon, but Georgie and I have been toiling night and day to prepare for the showcase," her brother answered with a weary smile.

"Ah, yes." Clara pursed her lips before assuming a benign expression. "Such an unexpected opportunity, and barely two weeks to prepare. You must be exhausted."

"Our department is stretched rather thin with the students and alumni preparing to show their work. I'm supervising three of the exhibitor teams myself and assisting Georgie whenever I am able. But a few sleepless nights are nothing compared to what this could do for Lovelace University. The Crystal Palace, Clara! It's a dream!"

The exhibition of inventions was intended to showcase the school's legacy, 15 years after its founding. Professor Sewell had been among the first students at the women's university and had long fought for her department's scholars to be recognised among Britain's finest by the academic societies. She had finally won her chance. But at what cost?

"A grand opportunity," Clara replied. "You received Captain Buchanan's dinner invitation, yes? I hope you will find the time to join us tomorrow eve."

"Of course! Georgie is terribly excited. She speaks highly of Captain Buchanan. It's very generous of her to offer to host our party. An excellent occasion to relax for an evening amid the commotion." Then he winced, "But was it truly necessary to invite everyone involved in mounting the exhibition?"

"Whatever do you mean?" Clara asked.

"I mean the exhibition's sponsor, Admiral Flint."

"Oh dear," Clara said, stifling a smile. "Have you found some competition, brother?"

Archie scowled. "It's no matter—that is, I'm rather of a mind to be jealous. He finds some excuse to speak with Georgie daily on some matter or another. But I know for a fact that no man could ever come between her and her research."

"Archie, my lad," piped Trick. "This is tragic. Has Georgie shown interest in the fellow? Did she share her ring spanner with him?"

"Hardly," he scoffed. "Georgie would never share her ring spanner."

Clara laughed, "Well, we don't wish to keep you from your work. Do pass on our congratulations to the Professor and her colleagues. We look forward to dining with them tomorrow."

With a quick hug goodbye, Archie was off and rambling across the lawn.

"Any news?" Trick asked, once they were alone.

"To the airship," she said, taking in their surroundings. "We have much to discuss."

The afternoon was spent in close conversation with Trick as the pair looked over the latest correspondence from Master Tims and his network of shopkeepers and spies.

A large map took up most of the starboard wall in the captain's quarters. It was not as detailed as the one she'd observed aboard the *Fregata*—Captain Buchanan's atlas had information on the prevailing winds and currents, seasonal shifts and atmospheric conditions. This one was simple geography, not unlike the maps of yesteryear, except the distances were measured in aeronautical miles.

Clara marked the positions of the pirate crews with coloured pins. She calculated the time it would take each crew to make it to London if a message were sent. It would depend on the weather, their airships, their fuel and their pilots. Madge and her raiders were hitting the major ports now, taking greater risks. Clara had sent instructions to drop the ruse of inspecting shipments and play up their piratical reputation a little, to further the stories and sightings of a red-haired captain and lend strength to the deceit that the Captain Duke and Olivier were not one and the same. With each decision, she had to weigh their mission against the risk that they would miss the next chance to rescue him. Every crew was now within a half day's flight to London, ready to rally to her side or to be dispatched to any corner of the country once they found him. She hoped it would be enough.

Trick and Mouse had packed everything that remained at Archie's Kendrick Road house in Reading. There were logbooks and receipts, and the missives too sensitive to be sent over the wireless. Clara pulled a loose sheet from the pile of letters, etched with a symbol they believed was connected to the Admiral and the rogue faction of Tradists: An old navigational tool over the diagram of a heart.

Master Tims had seen it on the Tradist ships that surveyed the wreckage of the Haven. Peg had sent word of high-ranking Tradist officials pinning it to their lapels. But with no further leads, the matter had been set aside as they focused their efforts on finding the Captain Duke.

Later that evening, after the small London crew had feasted together in celebration of their officer's return to health, Trick entertained them with his violin. Scales first, then simple melodies, and soon the heart-wrenching strains of his original compositions as he wielded the bow with deft precision. Clara was pleased to see his disposition so improved. But the Captain Duke's absence weighed on him, as it did them all.

Stop the Tradists. Save the Captain Duke.

Clara murmured the refrain to herself as she prepared for sleep. It was both a mission and a promise; a vow she intended to fulfill with haste.

Chapter 7: In which our heroine attempts diplomacy over dinner

"I would like to register my objection, Quartermaster."

The household staff of Captain Buchanan's house in Chelsea were bustling to and fro in the preparations for that evening's dinner. Cat and Clara were alone in the guest suite Marie had generously offered for their use. Clara was pinning her brown curls into a simple yet elegant twist, while Cat watched from her perch on the windowsill, drumming her fingernails in annoyance.

Clara's lip twitched into the glimmer of a smile. "I would be most pleased to hear it, Cat."

"I know the value of the information we are seeking to gather at the dinner tonight, and I, too, wish to figure out the missing connection so we can return to our search for the Captain," Cat began, while Clara grappled with a particularly stubborn pin. "But why all this talk when we could simply kidnap the Admiral and force him to explain himself and his plans?"

Clara sighed, and turned to look at her younger friend. Six years separated them. Cat would be sixteen next June, as she often reminded any who would listen. And she had started to demand a sound rationale for the orders she received.

Clara was inclined to indulge her, as she found in her a kindred spirit. Cat had an inquisitive mind that resisted simple explanations and challenged conventions.

That same desire for greater things was present in each of her friends. Nessa had been a dressmaker's apprentice before taking to the skies as a pilot. The Captain Duke chose to go beyond the laws of the land to help those in need. Even Archie and Professor Sewell were imagining a new world into existence by the power of their inventions. But each of them had sacrificed much to live as they pleased. This next generation would not be bound by the same customs. Cat would soar higher and farther than Clara could dream, and it made her heart glad.

Still, there were times when she was duty-bound to keep her young pilot in check, such as when she was proposing to kidnap a dinner guest. Clara imagined writing to her former etiquette instructor with such a question. Ecru napkins with an ivory tablecloth were enough to send Miss Ellington into convulsions. The matter of whether extracting sensitive information was an activity best suited to appetizers or dessert would send her to bed with the vapours.

Clara ran her fingers over the wooden combs in her lap. They were polished smooth, inlaid with opals. She held them out to Cat, who slid them into her hair, judging her work to be satisfactory with a nod. Clara stood and turned to place a hand on Cat's shoulders.

"I think you already know my response. We must think farther ahead than our immediate crisis. We have found ourselves in the eye of a storm whose magnitude we are still discovering. I understand your desire to take action, to take on the enemy in front of you. But we must be more farsighted than this. Perhaps a diplomatic solution will present itself. Perhaps the danger is greater than we know.

We will decide on our course of action when we have a clearer picture of who or what we stand against."

Cat huffed, "I suppose I agree with you. I just wish there was more I could do than be banished upstairs. If I wore a wig, perhaps? I swear they will not recognise me."

"You have done more than enough. It was your quick thinking that led to our discovery of the connection between Admiral Flint and the Professor. We each have a role to play in this plan. You'll have your chance soon. Tonight, it is mine."

Clara patted her hair to check that everything was in place and adjusted her voluminous skirts. She had determined that the occasion called for more formal attire than her usual regalia and was pleased to have an opportunity to wear more of Mrs. Cottingham's creations.

Dressed and ready for battle, Clara took a deep breath, straightened her spine, and descended the curved staircase to the party below.

It was a fine thing to see the pilots and professors mingling in the grand foyer. Captain Marie Buchanan had the evening well in hand, a resplendent hostess, greeting the guests and making introductions as necessary with an ease that Clara admired. While her own long-suffering etiquette instructor had managed to impart some knowledge of social graces, she had been reluctant student. However, Clara was first to admit the lessons had been of surprising benefit in her life as a pirate. She nodded to Marie and Nessa before joining Trick and his growing coterie of admirers as he showed off his new arm.

It was a quarter hour more before Professor Georgina Jameson Sewell appeared in the doorway, skirts swishing about her mechanical leg. At her side was Admiral Flint, with Archie following unhappily behind. Clara excused herself from the throng of engineers surrounding Trick—her exit barely made a ripple as the women closed ranks—and crossed the room to greet her brother. She caught part of Professor Sewell's discussion with Marie.

"…such an excellent opportunity if you ever wish to visit us in Reading. The aeronautics department who would be ever so pleased to have you as a guest lecturer."

"How delightful! I think that could be arranged," Captain Buchanan replied with a warm smile. "I know I am certainly eager to see more of your work. How are the preparations for the exhibit coming along?"

"The space is magnificent! But there is much to be done if we are to be ready by the weekend. Oh, but do not mistake me, we are quite glad of the opportunity to rest for an evening. I think we all needed a break from our endeavours these last few weeks."

"Then you are most welcome indeed. I am happy I could assist in this small way," said Captain Buchanan, before turning to greet the latest arrivals.

The guests shifted their attention from examining Trick's new arm to heap praises on its inventors. Archie and Professor Sewell swirled happily around, basking in the acclaim for their innovative design, each determined to assign the other the greater credit. Clara noticed the Admiral standing apart from the group, elbowed aside by the eager acolytes. He was frowning as he observed them, though he made a show of concern with the state of cleanliness of the mantle.

"It is quite the thing, is it not, Admiral Flint? Amazing

to behold the achievements of our modern technology," Clara remarked.

"A distraction," he stated flatly, before looking beyond her to address one of the male pilots in attendance. "It is folly to overextend the feminine mind on such a plaything. Her finite energies ought to be better used."

Clara found herself at a loss for words at the Admiral's slight. The other pilot did his best to disentangle himself from the conversation, but Flint had already clapped a hand on his shoulder to lead him away.

"I see you have become acquainted with Admiral Flint," a warm voice spoke from behind Clara. "Pay him no mind, he is poor company when not the center of focus."

Clara turned with a smile, "Mrs. Branson-Honeycutt! I'm so pleased you could join us."

After an exchange of the usual pleasantries, they retreated to a window seat with a good view of the action as they waited for dinner to be announced. The two women watched with humour as the Admiral did his best to remain within the vicinity of Professor Sewell without giving up his affectation of ennui.

"I find it curious, that he is a primary sponsor of this showcase," Clara mused. "Admiral Flint does not strike me as a passionate supporter of women's education."

"Strange, is it not?" remarked the elder socialite. "Though I think, perhaps, his motivations lie elsewhere. The man is rumoured to be in line for a cabinet position—Minister for Trade, if my sources are correct, with a peerage of his own." Then Mrs. Branson-Honeycutt leaned closer and adopted a conspiratorial tone, "But a position such as that comes with duties best handled with the assistance of a spouse, and the Admiral has not been moved by such inclinations of the marital sort."

"How tragic," Clara said in mock concern. "But to be granted a peerage? He must have truly distinguished himself."

"Well, his proposal to station soldiers on the merchant airships is being credited with stopping piracy of the skies. There have been far fewer reports of pirate attacks since early summer, and none this harvest season."

Clara did her best to maintain a neutral expression, "Why would the Admiral trouble himself with pirates?"

"Why indeed?" Mrs. Branson-Honeycutt replied.

Before Clara could press her for further details, the bell was rung for dinner and the company went through.

All was fair in war and seating arrangements. Captain Buchanan took her place at the head of the table, and Admiral Flint was accorded a seat of reasonable distinction near the foot with Nessa and Clara—easier to press him for information, with the added benefit of isolating him from Professor Sewell and Archie. Clara took some pleasure in his discomfort at the academic chatter forced upon him by his seatmate, an exuberant young woman studying the field of microbiology.

There were a number of students and professors from Lovelace in attendance, along with alumni who had achieved greatness after their studies. Professor Khadijah Sha'rawi was a recent addition to the faculty of mathematics. She had earned her degree at Lovelace before returning to Cairo for a number of years. Lady Alyxandra Sydenham, an heiress of modest means, had begun her own enterprise perfecting a dishwashing solution that could clean dishes without damage to hands. She had tripled her family's fortune and married her chauffeur, prompting a scandal which only served to further her renown. And there were star pupils in attendance, like Dorota Skłodowska. She had begun her education in biochemistry at an underground university in Poland before earning a scholarship to Lovelace alongside her younger sister, Maria. All were in good humour, catching up with friends and sharing the trials and tribulations of their latest works preparing for the exhibition.

"How are you adjusting to Lovelace, Professor Sha'rawi? Do you find it much changed since your return?" Lady Sydenham inquired, as the soup course was taken away.

"The expanded campus took some adjustment—I could spend days wandering the halls of the new library—but the weather is unfortunately just as I remembered," Professor Sha'rawi teased.

"Lovelace has benefitted immensely from the exchange program with Cairo. Many families are sending their daughters abroad to us thanks to your efforts," said Professor Sewell.

"We are happy to be at peace now," Professor Sha'rawi noted with a wide smile. "It has afforded so many opportunities for travel and study."

"And we are learning much from you as well," the elder Miss Sklodowska chimed in. "The Flying University only started in earnest last year, but you give me hope that one day our efforts will be rewarded with greater peace and prosperity for all."

Professor Sha'rawi accepted the compliment with grace,

"My dream is to further these efforts to educate and inform, perhaps even start a campus in Alexandria."

"I have heard great things about that ancient city," said Archie. "Tales of the magnificent library that once stood on the shores."

"Yes, and may it one day rise from the ashes as a beacon once more. The city is rebuilding anew after the bombardment. Perhaps, now that stability has been restored under the Khedive, we may rebuild the great library too."

"Admiral Flint, you travelled to Egypt, did you not?" Professor Sewell asked across the distance. "Have you seen Alexandria?"

The Admiral looked irritated at her attempt to include him in the conversation, and wiped his mouth on his napkin before replying. "I did not have the luxury. My posting was near the canal."

"Well, you must visit again now that the conflict is passed. Egypt is thriving," noted Professor Sha'rawi.

"Naturally. A war is good business," said the Admiral, as he took a bite of mutton.

"Oh?" she replied, her congenial expression fading.

The assembled company turned to look at him, their faces a mixture of curiosity, displeasure and shock.

"Well, yes. War builds empires. Industry is revived, young men are given purpose and employment. It can change a man. Discipline, order, fraternity."

"And what of the carnage that follows?" Lady Sydenham spoke up. "There are alternatives to war, and innovations that do not require a debt of blood to flourish and succeed."

"Indeed. Imagine a soldier that could not be maimed or killed, one that would never run from the battlefield or throw down his arms in fear. Have you served?" he asked, directing his attention to Trick.

The pirate was glaring, and Clara—fearing that he might decide to use the opportunity to offer some discipline of his own, gave a minute shake of her head. Trick took a bite of food, chewed and swallowed before giving his reply. It would be the height of incivility to speak with food in one's mouth after all.

"I've won my share of battles," Trick answered, flexing his arm. "But no, I have not had the privilege."

The Admiral sniffed, "Too much peace and a nation turns to sloth. Idle men turn to vice or become bookish and womanly."

He delivered this statement with an authoritative finality, before returning to his diligent mastication. Clara noticed a distinctive narrowing of eyes from the other women assembled. The silence stretched.

Then Archie spoke.

"Speaking of books, Professor Sewell has an extraordinary personal library, if I do say so myself. Professor Sha'rawi, I would recommend perusing her collection if you are interested in translations of some of the finest Arabic scholars. I have been most privileged to borrow a number of them."

"Archie is too modest. My shelves are fit to burst with the many texts he has lent me in return," added Professor

Sewell. "Please, Professor Sha'rawi, do feel free to visit at any time during your stay here. And you must inform me of any texts I ought to have in my collections."

"I would be quite happy to add my recommendations," Professor Sha'rawi replied, nodding her head in gratitude.

The assembly happily returned to discussion of texts, tomes and translated variants. But Clara felt the atmosphere of the room shift, with a deliberate effort by all to preserve the jubilant ambiance. Only the Admiral remained stiff and unyielding in the face of the others' irrepressible gaiety.

After the plates were cleared and all had their fill of the plentiful desserts, the company retired to the drawing room to rest amid the plush couches and overstuffed chairs while Trick provided the entertainment.

"I must say, I am thrilled to see how Mr. Killarney's treatment has progressed. He is a new man," Clara commented, during the break between songs.

Professor Sewell beamed, "Oh indeed! Mr. Whittington and I have made such progress in his rehabilitation. You see, Admiral Flint, how thrilling the field of biomechanical engineering is in its potential applications."

Admiral Flint paused with his tumbler suspended halfway to his mouth, before setting it on a table at his side, "I am not certain I understand the utility of turning one's appendage into an instrument."

"It was actually an extraordinary breakthrough," replied the Professor, leaning forward in her seat. "To capture the movement of the bow, we had to innovate a number of transradial controls and attachment mechanisms, and we are discovering improvements with every model. Mr. Killarney has been an exemplary subject to work with, and our work will help countless others. In fact, I would like to feature our work with Mr. Killarney at the exhibition. With his consent, of course," she added, gesturing to Trick. He extricated himself from the throng of admirers to join their group.

Professor Sewell clasped her hands and looked between Archie and Trick, "It would be the pinnacle of the grand opening, a live demonstration blending art and science, spectacle and scholarship in one. You would perform in the Crystal Palace for all of London's finest and brightest minds."

Clara could see the others' expressions matched her own surprise. Archie bore a mixture of confusion and hope. And Trick…he looked as though he had been struck. But before she could object to the Professor putting him on the spot, he began to laugh.

"Well, I say. What a capital idea. Imagine, Clara. I am to be famous. Do you think they'll take a photograph for the paper? Never mind, let's make certain that they do."

"I have no doubt of the extraordinary nature of your work, Professor." Admiral Flint interrupted, "I only hope your work with Mr. Whittington does not prove to be a distraction. There are other matters that require your attention."

The Professor tilted her head, "Admiral Flint, Mr. Whittington is my research partner."

"This was not part of our agreement," the Admiral bristled.

"Our agreement specifically enshrines my academic liberties in this matter," she replied. "My work with Mr. Whittington and Mr. Killarney is the most exemplary display of our department's capabilities by far. They are an essential component of the work I will be presenting to the Society during the exhibition."

Admiral Flint frowned, casting a glance to the crowded room, "We will discuss this in private."

"My decision is quite final." Professor Sewell smiled, showing her teeth.

Clara was reminded that this was a woman who established herself as an authority in her field of research before reaching the age of majority. More than ever, Clara wanted Professor Sewell to be an ally, not an adversary. At the very least, they could count on the Professor to speak her own mind. Clara was searching for an opportunity to press the Admiral further when he unexpectedly turned to her.

"Did you find yourself refreshed by your recent trip to the continent, Miss Whittington?"

After a moment's confusion, Clara recalled her alibi. Though she had left the Isle of Wight—and her broken engagement—by means of the nearest airship and found her way to the Captain Duke, it had been put about that she had been visiting cousins in France.

"Oh, yes. It was very…enlightening," she replied.

"I was pleased to see you in such good health at Mrs. Branson-Honeycutt's," he continued, with a nod to the woman. "You appear to make new friends easily. But I imagine you must be eager to return to the Isle of Wight and your fiancé."

Out of the corner of her eye, she saw her brother begin to rise from his seat.

"I beg your pardon," Clara spoke with a calmness that belied her racing heart. "You must not have heard. Mr. Corring and I are no longer betrothed."

"That is news to me indeed," said Admiral Flint, his expression unreadable. "My sincere apologies. I hope I did not cause offense."

"Not at all," she replied, with a tight smile.

"Do you expect you shall remain in London then?" the Admiral sneered, "To spend time with your…new friends?"

The hair on the back of Clara's neck rose as the nature of his inquiry became apparent. The Admiral had witnessed her talking with the Captain Duke as Olivier at the party. But something else nagged at her. They knew Alexander Corring was an associate of Admiral Flint. And her former intended must know that she would contradict his claims. What possible motivation could he have to perpetuate this pretense of an engagement?

Mrs. Branson-Honeycutt interjected, "I do hope you will, Clara. You made quite an impression at my little fête. I have heard nothing but tales of your charm and grace."

Clara blushed, "It was my pleasure. You have so many interesting companions."

"There was one in particular who caught your eye," teased Professor Sewell. "A handsome young man—Olivier, if I recall."

"Did you not hear?" asked Clara, letting her eyes grow wide. "He disappeared that very evening. No one has seen nor heard from him. Nessa and I were to take tea with him the Tuesday after and we found his household in a desperate state."

"How dreadful!" said Professor Sewell, with seemingly genuine concern in her eyes. "I do hope he is found safe."

"I have known Olivier for many years," added Mrs. Branson-Honeycutt. "My heart has been heavy since learning of his disappearance. I hope he is merely called away for an expedition, and not anything more serious. He's a good man, and a true friend."

The Admiral was silent while observing this exchange. He stood, suddenly, folding his hands behind his back, "If you will excuse me, the hour grows late and I have other matters to attend to."

"Interesting man," said Archie, after the door had shut behind him.

"Indeed," said Professor Sewell, with a curious look. "I had hoped to gather your opinion of him, though I fear it is already set. He is an awkward sort of fellow, I do hope you won't hold it against him."

"My opinion?" asked Archie.

"Well, as you know, I am better with machines than people," she said, before waving the matter away.

Trick began to muse aloud, "Let's see, two days to prepare… I have some of my own music I've been working on, but I can put together some favourites for the crowd, too. Could we get an orchestra? Just a wee one, only a dozen performers or so. I'll arrange it all."

The Professor beamed, "Of course! Anything you require."

Trick was grinning ear to ear, and Clara found herself laughing softly at the marked difference in her dear friend.

She found it difficult to recall the need for suspicion. She could not cast aspersions on the Professor's intentions, least not when confronted by such an obvious and genuine display of her kindness. Trick thanked her prodigiously before crossing the room to take up his instrument and play a cheerful tune of his own composition.

Archie touched the Professor on her arm and she turned to look up at him.

"You have changed that man's life, Georgie."

"Oh, Archie. I could not dream of achieving this without you at my side. That is—what I mean to say is, I want us to be partners, Archie Whittington."

"And so we are."

"What? That's—oh, yes. Research partners, but also... in business. As well. There is so much work to be done. And the Admiral has agreed to provide the means to do so."

Archie's hopefulness faded to confusion, his brow knit with concern.

"Archie, do not look so troubled. Won't it be splendid? We would have total freedom. With this funding, we can research anything our hearts desire!"

"And this Admiral, what role will he play in all of this?" Archie asked.

Professor Sewell frowned, "Well, he's an investor."

"An investor? And does he expect a say in our affairs?"

"Well, I imagine he may have some suggestions," she replied, standing to face him.

"Georgie," Archie began, before sighing and reaching out a hand. "You saw his behaviour tonight. I do not trust his intentions. I know you chafe at the constraints of academia sometimes, but these Tradists think of profit before all. What if these 'suggestions' become demands? I am certain this is an incredible opportunity—I believe you, I depend on your enthusiasm, always. But let us exercise some caution."

"Oh, Archie. Admiral Flint is a fine man, lauded for his conduct on the battlefield. He has been a tremendous ally in my work to help those veterans who have been disabled by illness or injury."

"Well, as far as this Admiral is concerned, I will need time to consider the matter," he said, though his serious expression gave way to a beaming smile as he took her hands. "But to work with you? Forever and always, yes."

The two academics made quite the pair standing together, hands clasped as they stared into each other's eyes, both looking as though they had found their own perfect pocket of the world to inhabit, the sole occupants of a shared universe. The scene tugged at Clara's heart, and reminded her of her purpose.

The party continued long beyond the hour of the Admiral's abrupt departure. Many hardly noticed his absence at all except to remark that the room had grown considerably brighter. But while Trick entertained the company with another song, Clara stole upstairs.

Cat and Mouse were already dressed and waiting with their packs.

"Now?" asked Cat.

Clara replied with a nod. "It's time to call the crews.

Send word as soon as you are able. Be safe and stay out of sight."

The sibling pirates wore matching grins as they slipped through the window and into the dark night.

Chapter 8: In which our hero is fortunately mistaken

His new lodgings were far less comfortable than the Captain Duke's previous accommodations. He had spent nearly a week in the gloomy cellar, where the air was rank with the scent of dried herbs and root vegetables fresh from harvest, and he was decidedly displeased with the arrangement. Only the dust motes moved, drifting through the late afternoon light streaming through the single, barred window.

The tranquillity ended abruptly as the trapdoor leading up to the kitchens opened, spilling more light from above as footsteps hurried down the narrow stairs. The Captain Duke took a breath and steeled himself for another interrogation. But this time, the big-eared guard sent to retrieve him was pale as a ghost and sweating nervously.

"Speak only when spoken to, if you know what's good for you," he said, binding the Captain's hands behind his back and shoving him up the steps.

Before he could take stock of his new surroundings, a cloth sack was drawn over his head. He heard angry voices, as he was led down a hallway and into another room. He made a show of bumping into the wall and against the doorway, counting his steps and judging the breadth of the passageways in case there was an opportunity for escape.

"The reports cannot be correct. We have the pirate right here."

"And yet, I continue to receive word of sightings in the western airbours."

The Captain felt a faint stirring of memory. Where had he heard that voice before? The voices quieted as he crossed the threshold and was forced into a chair.

"You see, sir? We picked him up in the docklands, just where our contact said he would be."

"Show me."

"Sir, are you certain? We would not wish to risk—"

"Now, Corring."

The Captain Duke blinked against the light as the covering was removed, focusing his gaze on the room and its occupants. They were in a drawing room, with forest green walls and threadbare carpet. The furniture looked new, but well-made, upholstered in stripes of mint and cream. He made note of which elements would be useful in a fight. Two captors stood at his elbows, a third a few feet away. But all had directed their attention to the man standing by a large writing desk in the corner.

"Admiral Flint?" said the Captain Duke, adopting a tone of bemusement. "Whatever are you doing here?"

The Admiral took in his disheveled appearance, the fine clothes he wore to Mrs. Branson-Honeycutt's salon—and turned on the one with the moustache in shock and fury, taking him by the collar and shoving him into a wall.

"You fool. You layabout. I was introduced to this

gentleman barely a fortnight ago by our esteemed Professor Sewell. In the home of Mrs. Branson-Honeycutt no less, while the pirate and his crew were witnessed plundering the northwest. I knew when you sent word that you had captured our adversary that it was too convenient to be an honest account. But this—this is truly beyond the pale."

The man looked around him in desperation, but none of his henchmen looked eager to speak in his defence. They seemed to shrink in the presence of their commander, each doing his best to escape notice.

"With all due respect, sir, I thought it prudent to conduct a more thorough interrogation of the pirate myself before concerning you with this trivial affair."

"A trivial affair? You kidnapped a private citizen!"

"No, sir, believe me. This man is a scoundrel. A liar and a thief!"

The Admiral released him in disgust, turning his back and pinching the bridge of his nose before continuing his tirade. "He was also sighted in the company of your alleged fiancée. Is that what this is?" he asked, gesturing toward the Captain Duke. "Some poor show at vengeance for a slight to your honour? I fear you have allowed your passions to cloud your judgement."

"Miss Whittington suffers from a fit of nerves. We will be wed when she has recovered," he protested.

Suddenly, the Captain Duke was glad for the shackles around his wrists. Never had he felt so strong a compulsion to strike a man. This was the man who had deceived Clara and her family. This was the man who caused her to flee her home to protect the ones she loved. This was the man who pretended to lay claim to her hand despite her protestations.

"I had the misfortune of dining with her and her milksop of a brother yesterday eve. The lady has a very different opinion on the matter. Having met her, I cannot say I understand your preoccupation. Did you think her fortune would save you?" Admiral Flint continued.

The Captain Duke felt a rush of hope. Clara was safe.

Alexander Corring's eyes flicked between the Admiral and the Captain, his expression desperate, "We had the right tallport, Thompson said—"

"Thompson this, Thompson that. Your man is a dunderhead."

"That I will readily admit," said Corring. "But he swore to me that he saw the Captain Duke in London."

"And where is he now? Bring forth this Thompson, have him attest to the pirate's identity."

Corring had taken on a faint sheen of sweat and was decidedly grey in pallor. "He is gone, sir. He left on a charter for Australia."

The Captain Duke hid a smile. He could almost admire the cowardly Thompson for double-crossing him and his crew. They had spared his life after all upon capturing the gunpowder ship he had captained, taking Clara as a crewmate in the process. Despite Nessa's threats, Thompson must have perceived Admiral Flint as a more fearful figure, he noted—an adversary to be wary of.

"You disappoint me, Corring. I cannot have you jeopardising our designs, not this close to seeing our plan to fruition. You leave me no choice…"

"Wait! Wait, I can prove that he is the pirate. I have

another source," Corring replied. "Give me a week, and I will have the evidence you require."

While the Admiral considered his request, the Captain Duke finally spoke.

"Admiral, sir. My name is Marmaduke Ivan Lysander Olivier. As you said, we met in the home of Mrs. Branson-Honeycutt. I can prove I am who I say I am. If this is a case of mistaken identity, free me from these fools and I'll consider this entire affair to be forgotten."

"Forgotten, you say? Be that as it may, you do bear a striking resemblance to the description of the man we seek," Admiral Flint replied, before turning his attention to Corring. "You have three days. I have a delivery to make in London, where we will advance our scheme thanks to the efforts of the Professor."

"Very well, sir. What would you have us do with him until then?"

"Keep him bound. When I return, you had better have your proof—or you'll be the one wearing those chains. I need that pirate."

Admiral Flint left, with barely a glance over his shoulder towards the very man he sought.

His captors hauled him from the chair and retraced their steps toward the kitchen cellar. As he began to descend the narrow stairs, Corring grabbed him by the shirt, pulling him off balance.

"You may have fooled the Admiral, but you will never deceive me. I cannot imagine what my fiancée saw in such a scoundrel."

"You aren't worthy of her," the Captain Duke seethed. "And you never will be. No gentleman requires the subjugation of another to feel himself a man."

"I never claimed to be a gentleman," sneered Corring, before giving him a shove. Bound as he was, the Captain Duke fell head over heels down the steps into the dark. He heard the sound of heavy footsteps follow and recoiled as the first blow caught him in the ribs.

The last thing he remembered—as his attacker retreated and the door to his makeshift cell was shut—was the faint spectacle of twin shadows outlined against the night, peering down through the cellar's single window.

Chapter 9: In which our heroine turns to face the oncoming storm

Clara had never been to the Crystal Palace. Her family had always intended to go, before her father's illness. Now her brother's work would be showcased within its venerated court. She took a deep breath as she stepped out of the small ferryair transport they had taken to Sydenham and saw the building and surrounding park stretching out before her.

Four double-tiered tallports flanked an entryway leading up past a reservoir to the famed fountains and gardens. Visitors were already arriving to enjoy the grounds before the great opening of the exhibit. Clara could see couples and families taking a stroll around a small lake, whose islands recalled pleasing memories of the Haven before the gunpowder incident. The path to the main building was framed by fountains, some sending water jetting high into the air while others created pleasant cascades that rippled alongside the walkway. Rose gardens spiralled along circular footpaths shaped to resemble cogs and gears. And the Crystal Palace towered above it all.

The building was the pinnacle achievement of the Great Exhibition of 1851, and had been imitated far and wide. It was made of glass and iron, stacked many stories high in an architectural feat of modern innovation. The palace gleamed in the midday sun as a gem, a shining symbol of possibility. Some even called it the keystone of the age of invention, its unveiling an unparalleled celebration of technology that set

Great Britain on a path to unmatched engineering prowess. For 35 years, the exhibits shown within had celebrated the accomplishments of every corner of the empire, from Australia to India to Canada. The Lovelace University showcase was to formally open that afternoon with Trick's concert, leaving plenty of time to explore.

As Clara entered the central transept, an usher provided her with a handbook filled with illustrations and commentary on the current exhibits. A beautiful, scrolling title declared "On the Occasion of the 15th Anniversary of the Establishment of Lovelace University." Clara flipped through the pages as she walked into the light-filled space. After an introduction detailing the university's founding by the heirs of Ada Lovelace and the renowned scientist Mary Somerville, there was a brief note to highlight the work of Professor Georgina Jameson Sewell and Sir Archibald Whittington in the field of biomechanical engineering, accompanied by an illustration of their design for Trick's new arm.

Clara felt a surge of pride. They had begun their task in sorrow, with the loss of the Haven and Trick's melancholy. And now they were about to unveil their achievement to the world. She only wished the Captain and their crew could be here to see it as well. She checked the map and made her way to the hall where the Lovelace students were to exhibit their work.

A heavy velvet rope was strung to block entry to the gathering crowd of curious onlookers, eager for their first peak at the wonders within. A gangly sentry was doing his best to deter them. Clara marched straight to the front and lifted her chin to look him in the eye.

"Clara Whittington. I am expected," she said, arching her eyebrow.

The excuses died on his lips as he hurried to let her through. Clara stifled a smile and gave a simple nod as she passed.

The hall was organized by field of study. Posters lined the walls, profiling notable graduates of the school and their innovations in medicine, engineering, astronomy and the arts. Taking after its namesake, the university had encouraged its students to be multi-disciplinary in their pursuits. The poetry of mathematics could be seen in many of the students' works, including a replica of the Lovelace-Babbage Analytical Engine. Other displays had tiny autobauble engines to power their contraptions, like a mechanism to polish floors and another machine to automate the kneading of dough. The section on medical innovations was curtained off so as not to offend those of delicate sensibilities—here was the life-saving work to better understand women's labours in childbearing.

Clara's spirits were lifted higher with each marvel. But she paused as she came across a curious specimen on a dais near the back of the hall. It was massive, twice her height with four pistons the size of tree trunks for legs. The lines of the machine spoke of the Professor's handiwork, but the weaponry sent chills down Clara's spine. Empty ammunition belts twisted around the core of the machine, feeding large cannons that could rotate in any direction. It sat inert, but gave the impression of menace all the same. This automaton design was not one of healing or expanding human capability—it was built to destroy.

This was the prototype the Admiral had spoken of, the one they intended to produce on a massive scale. Clara felt her mouth run dry, and she forced herself not to look back at the formidable weapon as she made her way across the hall to the amphitheatre.

"Clara, are you enjoying the exhibit?" Archie asked, his delight apparent as she approached.

"I—I need to speak to Trick," she replied. "Do you know where I can find him?"

Archie gave her a curious look but led her up a small set of stairs to the backstage. Clara waved greetings at the professors and students she recognized, following close on his heels. They went down a hallway and past a series of dressing rooms until they reached one with Mr. Killarney written on the name plate. A brief knock, and Trick called for them to enter. Inside, he stood before a long mirror, attempting to adjust his bow tie with his left hand. His dark hair was slicked back and his beard was neatly trimmed. He wore a suit with tails and a dashing crimson cummerbund over a crisp white shirt. The harness for his right arm, made with finely-tooled black leather and gold accents, shone in the light.

"Trick, you look splendid! May I?" she asked, before helping to adjust the tie.

"Quite sharp, if I do say so myself," added Archie.

Trick moved to sit before the dressing table and stroked the fine Pernambuco bow before fitting it into the attachment. He picked up the Tourte violin gifted to him by Lovelace and played some practice notes. Clara was fascinated by the delicate balance of gears that responded to Trick's every movement.

"Now, why don't you tell me what is troubling you so?" he said, once satisfied with the sound.

Clara glanced at her brother, before responding. "Did you see it?"

Trick took a deep breath, "Yes."

"Archie, did you know?" she asked.

"The automaton? It's only a prototype," he replied. "Georgie has asked me to work with her on refining this new application of her work to help injured soldiers. I know it looks fearsome, but it's harmless in its current state."

Clara narrowed her eyes. "Harmless? Have you seen it? It is inhumane by design. A literal killing machine. It is no mere model, it's a proof of concept." She rubbed her temples. Too many secrets. Not enough trust. She traded a look with Trick and turned to face her brother. "You know that Professor Sewell is working with Admiral Flint on this design. But Cat overheard them speaking of an army. They are planning to build more."

Archie rolled his eyes, "Clara, it would take more than the university's entire endowment to achieve such a thing. There is no way that Flint has those resources."

"He has a rogue faction of the Tradists working for him. There is some larger scheme at play—and he's connected to Alexander Corring and the men who kidnapped the Captain Duke. The Professor herself might be involved. I don't believe we can trust her."

"Explain yourself," he frowned.

"Think, Archie. She's not simply helping injured soldiers, they plan to replace them."

"It's true," added Trick. "A soldier that could not be injured or killed, that's what he said at dinner the other night. Does the Admiral seem to you as one who would support a showcase dedicated to women scholars out of pure intentions? As pleased as I am to be part of this, you know as well as I there is some ulterior motive at play. I think they intend to use this as an opportunity to legitimize their production of the automaton, perhaps even to garner support as they clear up regulatory entanglements."

Archie was silent, but his expression was one of shock. He looked to each of them before standing suddenly to pace the room.

"It can't be. She would never."

Clara pressed a hand to his arm. "Archie, if there is anything you know—anything that could help us put a stop to this, please."

"If Professor Sewell is involved, I am certain everything is above board," he answered, pulling away.

"Then you are convinced that in her quest for knowledge Professor Sewell has been purely ethical in the application of her innovations?" Clara snapped. "Archie, please."

"She would not risk Lovelace," he said, adamant. "She would never risk Lovelace."

"Mayhap she thinks she is helping. It looks to me as though the Admiral secured her commitment by using her devotion to the school."

"I trust her!" Archie shouted, before turning from them to speak in the barest whisper, "I love her, Clara."

"And the life of the man I love may rest in her hands."

The room was so still, Clara swore she could hear her own heartbeat pounding in her chest. Had she said the words aloud before? Her feelings felt tangible and rending, suddenly. As though she might break apart from the fear of never seeing her Captain again. Yet she also felt a gathering in her core, a fierce determination.

"We're going to stop the Tradists and save the Captain Duke," she said, lifting her chin. "Are you with us?"

Archie sat heavily, his head in his hands. He was quiet for some time before standing up, a wild look in his eyes. "Whatever your plan, you may always rely on my assistance."

Clara hugged her brother tightly, "Thank you."

"There's more. You told me of the gunpowder ship, the explosion at the Haven. I think I know what it was intended for. The prototype—the automaton—it is equipped with a new type of combustion power to automate the firing of its weapons. Georgie was arguing with the Admiral about supply chain issues and the need for further testing."

Clara let out a deep sigh, "If that is so, then we have inadvertently delayed the execution of the Tradist scheme. But we are running out of time. It sounds as though Corring has been holding them off with his promises to locate the missing shipment. They must know by now that it is lost forever. Stopping Professor Sewell may be our best chance to defeat Admiral Flint and the Tradists."

When Archie spoke, his voice was breathless and grim, as though he could hardly believe the words that issued from his mouth.

"Before you do anything, please let me speak with her. I can reason with her, I'm certain of it. And if I cannot…" He shook his head, before looking to Clara and Trick. "But today is for Lovelace. Let today be a day for celebration, please."

They nodded their assent. Archie excused himself, muttering about the follies of love and science.

Clara turned back to Trick with a heavy heart. "I am sorry. I know she has done a great deal for you."

"If anyone can bring the Professor to our side, it will be your brother. We'll let him try his way before we resort to ours," he replied.

"I saw that prototype and it struck me, the reality of what we are up against. People who hold so little value for human life that they seek new and more terrible means of ending it. And I cannot reconcile what I know of the Professor with such a view."

Trick patted his violin, "Then perhaps we must wait a little longer in our judgement of her."

Clara nodded soberly. She had to hope for her brother's success.

"Have you heard from Cat or Mouse?" Trick asked.

"Nothing yet. I have pilots monitoring the wireless. The crews are standing by, ready to fly to any corner of the country as soon as we receive word. I only hope that…"

She broke off, wringing her hands.

"Clara," Trick said, standing to place his hand on her shoulder. "You chose to trust in the skill of two of the finest pilots I have ever laid eyes on. Cat and Mouse may be young, but they have survived and thrived together. They are capable of this task. You'll see. Come, it is nearly time. You'll want to get a good seat and I must find my orchestra."

Clara squeezed her friends hand in reply. As she reached the door, she turned. "Trick! Break a leg."

"I'll run out of limbs," he said, with a jovial smile. "Thank you."

The crowd in the grand hall was milling about in their Sunday best, jostling for a view of the stage set up under a soaring atrium. Clara took her seat in the small reserved section, nodding to Mrs. Branson-Honeycutt in the next row. The chatter quieted somewhat once the speeches began—a lengthy introduction by the chief curator, Mr. Hodgson, and brief remarks acknowledging the historical occasion by Chancellor Seacole—but it was Trick's performance that spelled the room into silence.

He took the stage and bowed to the orchestra, the audience, and the dignitaries in attendance before raising his bow. The delicate gears and bearings of his prosthetic arm shone as he struck a pose and began to play at the conductor's signal.

His compositions had taken on a new depth since his injury. Clara's breath caught as he drew the haunting strains from his instrument, a song of loss and despair and the resilience to move on. The violin pierced the air and made the hearts of all who listened soar. When the last note trembled to a close, the room paused, held in rapture, before breaking into applause. Those who were not already standing rose from their seats.

Trick took their accolades in stride, bowing to the audience with a graceful flourish of his bow. Then, with a dashing grin, he launched into the next song, a raucous, uplifting caper.

Clara was clapping along with the rest when a hand gripped her elbow. She was startled, and immediately reached for the pistol concealed within her skirts.

"It's me, Clara," Nessa whispered into her ear.

Clara's heart caught as Nessa spoke the words she had been waiting to hear: "They found him."

Overcome with emotion, she struggled to maintain her composure.

"If we leave now, we can be there by nightfall," Nessa continued. "I've sent word ahead to Himmat to meet us, but we must not tarry."

"But Trick, Archie…we can't just leave," Clara said, gesturing to the stage, where Trick was still in the middle of his performance. Then she remembered her promise to Archie that today would be a day for celebration.

"Mrs. Branson-Honeycutt," she called as she turned around in her seat, grateful that Trick had chosen to perform some of the more boisterous numbers in his repertoire. "I have a personal matter to attend to, could you kindly tell my brother and Mr. Killarney I've been called away?"

"Of course, dear. Where shall I tell them you've gone?" the socialite asked, leaning forward in her seat.

Clara's mind raced as she considered her options. Could Mrs. Branson-Honeycutt be trusted? She looked to Nessa, who nodded in silent agreement.

"Home. Tell them I am going home."

Chapter 10: In which our heroine is determined to take the advantage

Alone in her cabin as the airship crossed the strait to the Isle of Wight, Clara knelt before the trunk at the end of the bed. Opening the lid, she lifted an intricate box from within, inlaid with a design of birds soaring above the clouds that she had purchased from a marquetry shop on Piccadilly. Pressing a hidden panel to release the latch, she opened it. Inside, resting on a bed of indigo that complemented their silver gleam: her father's matched duelling pistols.

Grief was an ache that did not fade. It only became familiar.

His long illness and death had marked her family in different ways. Her mother retreated from society life. Her brother had devoted himself to his studies. And Clara…

Before, she had looked to others to fill the gaping hole her father had left. To ease the feeling that she had lost all safety and security in the world. Now, she had but to look in the mirror.

And she did, as she fastened the leather holster around her hips, smiling at her reflection. Dark curls twisted back into a sensible plait. A simple blouse, rolled at the sleeves. She stood tall, her posture not of primness, but of strength. She felt powerful. She felt as though she had found her place in the world. Finally, she felt like herself.

The time for waiting had passed. Now they had their chance. Now was the time for action.

The airship docks in Newport were at the centre of the town, and she looked down on the familiar streets with longing. But sour faces greeted their arrival. Mouse hurried along the spoke of the tallport towards the airship as they landed with Himmat, looking worried, a tall turban of deep blue crowning his head.

"We have a bit of a problem," said Mouse, after greetings were exchanged.

"What is the matter?" Clara asked. "Did we miss him again? Is he hurt?"

"We've located the house where Corring and his men are holding the Captain," said Himmat. "But he is injured, locked in the cellar. And Corring is in a desperate state of mind, having lost the favour of Admiral Flint and the Tradists. We believe he was holding off his debtors with the promise of his engagement to you, and he intended to use the Captain Duke to make up for his failure in losing the shipment of gunpowder. We have been watching for activity, but thought it best to wait for your arrival, Quartermaster."

"Alexander Corring is not one inclined to face the consequences of his errors in judgement," Clara noted with irritation. "He'll be unpredictable."

Nessa let out her breath in a huff, "Rather inconvenient, that. Where is Cat?"

"She's posted nearby to keep an eye on things while I found Himmat and came to meet you," Mouse explained. "In case they move him again, or..."

Clara's eyes narrowed, and her hand drifted to one of the pistols at her side.

"I know a place where we'll be safe to regroup, I'll give you the coordinates. We do this tonight."

"How will we get in?" asked Nessa.

"The place is crawling with Corring's men," said Mouse.

Clara smiled, "We'll walk through the front door. I think it is time that Corring and I discussed our incompatible understandings on the matter of our engagement."

At the appointed hour, Clara marched to the front of the house with Nessa trailing in her wake and gave three sharp knocks on the door. It opened to reveal a confused young man with large ears.

"Good evening, missus. May I assist you in some way?"

"I am here to see Mr. Corring."

"Ah, Mr. Corring is… indisposed. What is your business with him?"

"Unfortunately, it cannot wait," Clara replied, brushing past him with a forceful push on the door. "Alexander!" she called.

"Wait! You can't—I beg your pardon, Miss. You must wait outside."

"I think not," Clara said as she flounced past the young man, shooting a glare over her shoulder with lethal intensity. "Tell him his fiancée is here."

It took a moment for his shock to register, but the man gave a small bow and scrambled up the staircase. In the drawing room, Clara righted an overturned chair and made herself comfortable, taking care that her voluminous skirt did not reveal the weapons secreted in its folds. Nessa stood at her back, gloved hands folded one over the other as they waited.

Corring entered the room with the measured steps of a drunkard. His face was pale and his hair had been smoothed back somewhat hastily from what Clara could tell, but he wore a dashing smile. Ignoring the unruly state of the house, he walked to the fireplace and posed himself artfully by the mantle before speaking.

"Clara, my heart. I did not expect to see you here," he said, bringing a hand to his chest.

Clara lifted her chin, "Alexander. You have been well, I trust?"

"Quite. How did you find your travels?" he asked with a pointed tone.

She smiled, "Refreshing."

The stilted conversation continued with the requisite pleasantries, neither speaker breaking their poise, as Clara drew out the uncomfortable situation for as long as she dared.

The plan was to make a scene and play the fainting maiden, sending Nessa for smelling salts while she distracted Corring and his men. Then, if all went well, Nessa could quietly free the Captain Duke and send him out the back stair. Clara and Nessa would leave with Corring none the wiser until they checked on their captive. The pirates were waiting at the edge of the town to fly them safely away.

Clara was, however, prepared for things to go less than perfectly.

"I must say. Delighted as I am by your visit, I do wish it were under better circumstances," Corring said, with affected indifference.

"Better circumstances?" she repeated, tilting her head.

With exaggerated nonchalance, he leaned against the wall and crossed his arms.

"I know why you are here."

"Oh?"

"You were sent here, weren't you? By the pirate. Don't act surprised, they told me all about his infatuation with you. Fear not, my dear. You will be safe with us." He crossed the room to kneel before her and took her hands in his own, "I will not let the villain take you again."

Clara's heart stilled, and she tried to pull her hands from his grasp, but his grip tightened around her wrists. She could feel Nessa tense behind her, preparing to strike.

"Alexander, you forget yourself," she hissed through clenched teeth, as she readied herself to break his grasp.

"Clara, Clara. I know how you must have suffered these past months. But no one need know of this lapse in judgement. I have told no one of your indiscretions and I am willing to overlook any defilement—if you honour our arrangement."

He released one of her wrists, but only to pull a ring from his pocket, the very same one that Clara had returned to him months before.

"I kept it, you see? I have kept it on my person all this time. I knew you would come back to me."

"I fear you are mistaken," said Clara, once she found her voice. "I came to request that you cease in your pursuit of my hand. I was quite clear about my wishes in my note to you. There are no circumstances under which I could be compelled to take your hand in marriage."

"If you had only come to me with your fears, this estrangement could have been avoided."

"If you had only been honest about your intentions, this engagement could have been avoided."

Clara kept her tone light, but she could see the impact of her words play out across Corring's face as he stiffened in surprise. His smile took on the characteristics of a sneer.

"Nonsense. Who else would have you now that you are ruined? Your dowry and inheritance are impressive, but it is not every man who would overlook piracy, no matter your degree of involvement. But you will be free of this pirate's influence soon, I swear it."

Alexander spoke sweetly but there was venom in his words.

A tepid knock at the door interrupted his tirade.

"Sir?"

"What?" he barked at the young man who peered inside.

"Ah, sir, you said you wished to know once we located the man—that is, I know you said you were not to be interrupted, but I thought it rather important—"

Corring left Clara's side and strode to the door to

rebuke his subordinate. He swung it open to reveal two of his men—with Robbie Codswaddle gagged and bound between them.

Three realizations came to Clara's mind with rapid clarity.

First, that in a few short months she had mastered the fear that once compelled her to flee her fiancé. Second, that Alexander truly appeared to believe she was allied with the pirates under duress. Third, that the presence of Robbie meant they were in imminent danger if she did not act with haste.

Clara quickly rose to stand at Nessa's side and readied for a fight. Abandoning all pretence, Clara pulled her pistols from beneath her skirts and aimed them squarely at Robbie.

Panic flashing in his eyes, Robbie heaved himself to the left, managing to get hold of one of his captors' pistols. As he fumbled in his attempt to fire into the drawing room, Corring sprang into action, thinking Robbie was aiming for himself. They grappled and toppled to the floor, Corring yelling out as he received an elbow to his spleen. Confusion reigned as the two guards struggled to subdue the traitorous former crewmate, and Clara and Nessa took their advantage. Nessa threw a small vial of Madge's concoction into the melee with perfect aim. The delicate filament in the center of the glass chamber broke, mixing the powder and liquid within. Dense blue smoke billowed outward to fill the room, as Clara and Nessa fled through an interior door. Wisps of smoke followed them down the hall, along with the muffled shouts and coughs of Corring and his men.

Clara and Nessa ran to the kitchens, finding them under guard by a single man who had no time to voice his shock as Nessa tackled and subdued him. Clara did not hesitate, ripping the keys from his belt and heaving open the trapdoor to the cellar, dashing down the narrow stairs into the darkness below.

She shut her eyes to adjust to the dimness as she descended; opening them once she felt her feet hit the firm earth, pistols out and ready to shoot.

There was a single figure in the cellar, crouched in the shadows in preparation for a fight as he shaded his eyes against the light. His hair was loose and tumbling over his shoulders. His shirt was half-buttoned and stained with drops of blood.

"Clara?"

In two strides, she was in his arms, fingers tangled in his hair as he kissed her, pressing her body against his own. The rush of adrenaline became something else entirely, a lightning bolt of electricity in her veins. The kiss deepened until it left them gasping for breath and laughing softly as the Captain leaned his forehead against hers.

"You're hurt," she said softly.

"Not when you kiss me like that," he murmured.

Then Nessa's voice rang out from above, "Not to disturb your reunion but we're about to have some unwelcome company."

Clara could not help her smile as she knelt to unlock his chains.

"Bruises only," he said. He gasped as Clara helped him to climb the stairs. "Alright, possibly a cracked rib. I've survived worse."

His breath was shallow, but they managed together. Nessa was waiting with a candle; she had snuffed all the lights in the kitchen. They made no sound as the three of them moved as one unit through the back entrance into the dark alley behind the house.

"Where are the others?" asked the Captain Duke, his arm around Clara's shoulder for support.

"Himmat is holding a position near the edge of town," said Nessa.

The Captain winced, "How far?"

The women traded looks. Clara could hear the ruckus growing in volume behind them, and knew they had but minutes to spare.

"Follow me, I know the way."

Clara's heart hammered in her chest, her mind focused on remembering Newport's intricate network of back lanes and alleyways as they made their way to the meeting point. The buildings cast deep shadows in the moonlit night. The Captain was pale and breathing heavily when they paused. With each passing moment, the sounds of the pursuit grew louder.

"Run, Clara," said the Captain, turning to her and cupping her face in his hands. "Leave now while you can."

She reached up to curl her fingers around his and looked into the eyes of her brave Captain Duke.

"No," Clara said.

"No?" he repeated, with a look of puzzlement.

Before he could protest further, Clara turned to Nessa.

"Here, cross your arms like so, quickly now, and clasp my wrists. We'll carry him. We need to run once we leave this cover."

"They'll see us!"

"Well, I'm hoping our crew sees us first."

The Captain shook his head, "It is too risky. Clara, Nessa, leave now. That's an order."

The shouts were barely two streets away.

"Like hell," Clara said, as they positioned themselves to scoop him up. "Hold our shoulders." Nessa and Clara linked their arms, and with the Captain secure, they ran.

It was awkward going at first, but they quickly fell into a steady rhythm. Months of training exercises under Nessa's careful tutelage had turned Clara's arms and legs to lean muscle, and her determination had never been stronger. She nearly broke her pace as she felt her pistol leave its holster—only to feel the impact of the recoil as the Captain Duke shot at one of their pursuers. They were discovered.

"Starboard aft!" the Captain called, his face pale from the effort.

Clara and Nessa quickly deduced his meaning and angled their sprint to give him better aim as he fired behind them. As soon as she caught sight of the river ahead of them, Clara threw all caution to the wind and yelled for the waiting crew. They must be close enough to see them by now!

For a heart-wrenching moment, she wondered if her pilots had been captured or forced to relocate. Clara searched the horizon as she ran, refusing to break the pace though her legs screamed for relief.

And then she saw the outline of a glider against the sky as Cat sailed into battle. Her pistol cracked as she dove towards the pursuit, an adolescent Valkyrie performing her aeronautic acrobatics with ease.

An airship rose above the rooftops, and a rope ladder was cast down from the side as it drifted towards their position. Releasing the Captain, Nessa reached the ladder first and held it steady it as Clara helped him climb. He was gasping from the effort, though he tried not to show his pain. Clara swung around to the opposite side and linked her arms with his, fearing that his injuries might cause him to lose his grip. She clung to him as the airship rose above the city with the three of them dangling beneath. Cat flew in sweeping arcs to guard their flank as the crew hauled them up with the ladder, leaving their pursuers cursing on the ground far below.

Chapter 11: In which our heroine finds her way home

The pirates flew north with the River Medina towards the Solent at Cowes, passing shiny new warehouses with half-constructed leisurecraft resting in the yards. When they felt certain they were beyond the sight of Corring and his men, they followed the shoreline east—towards Whittington Manor.

Clara's family home was set back from the nearest road, a paragon of Jacobean design, with generous windows, peaked roofs and chimneys that reached to the sky. Her grandfather had purchased the manor long ago as a wedding gift for his betrothed, hoping to fill its many rooms with children. They had but a single son, but they filled the home with love and kindness instead. Her heart turned over as happy memories flooded her mind.

The unruly garden had room enough for Himmat to land the aircraft amidst the untrimmed hedges. But as they disembarked, Clara made an unexpected discovery:

Lights were burning in the ground floor parlour, a beacon of comfort in the crisp autumn air—except no one was supposed to be home.

They entered in silence, the Captain Duke walking with his arm around Clara's shoulder. Nessa stayed close by their side, weapons drawn, while Himmat and the other pilots held the rear with Cat and Mouse. The Captain's breathing was shallow, though his colour had improved greatly on the journey. Clara could feel his warmth through the thin fabric of his shirt—one he still had not bothered to finish buttoning, she noted, before pushing the matter from her mind. Now was not the time to indulge in fantasies.

Low voices emanated from the parlour at the end of the hall. Placing a finger to her lips, Clara passed the Captain off to Nessa for support as she crept closer to the door. Reflected in the mirror above the fireplace, she could see her grandmother's silver tea service.

And on the armchair opposite…

"Mother!"

There was a clattering of teacups as Mrs. Whittington and her lady's maid leapt to their feet, startled by her exclamation.

"Clara, dear. We were not—oh, my heart! Welcome home!"

Mrs. Whittington recovered from her surprise and glided across the room to embrace her daughter. Her only reaction upon finding her armed and in the company of pirates, two children, and a half-dressed man was the barest twitch of an eyebrow and a warm smile.

"I was not expecting company. What a happy surprise! Mrs. Hutchins, do prepare more tea for our guests," she called over her shoulder. She gestured to the tea service. "You must forgive the appalling lack of sandwiches."

Clara remembered her manners, "Thank you, I—yes. Yes, tea. Mother, what are you doing here? I mean, at home? I thought you were visiting Aunt Henrietta in Paris?"

"Well, to be perfectly honest, your beloved aunt is a tedious woman to be around while in mourning. So I decided to end my trip early." She looked over Clara's shoulder to the Captain Duke and smiled brightly, "I must say, it was a tad lonesome with the house to myself. How kind of you to bring friends."

"Mother, may I introduce the Capt—ah, Mr. Olivier," Clara said, casting a desperate glance behind her.

Nessa shrugged. Cat and Mouse were barely stifling their laughter. The Captain Duke was far more accommodating of the unexpected circumstances. He stepped forward.

"Mrs. Whittington, thank you kindly for opening your home to my companions and I. We are in your debt," he said, with a slight bow, though it clearly pained him.

"Goodness!" cried her mother. "Are you injured? Shall I send for the physician?"

"No, no. You need not trouble yourself. It is nothing a good dose of rest cannot fix."

Mrs. Whittington took in his bloodied shirt, the tense looks being traded between the pirates. Then she looked to Clara, with a look of genuine curiosity and delight.

"Well then, you must convalesce here. I insist," she commanded, as she ushered them into the room. "Clara, do make our guests feel welcome. I'll have the staff prepare a snack and ready the guest bedrooms."

She kissed each of Clara's cheeks and whispered her gladness that she was home before bustling out of the room with Mrs. Hutchins to wake the cook and butler.

"Well. That was not the reception I expected," said Nessa, sinking into a chair.

"No? Mother has always delighted in interesting company. I'm certain we have exceeded her expectations in that regard," Clara replied with a small laugh. "There will be questions in the morning, but for now I suggest we enjoy the respite."

The Captain moved closer to murmur in her ear, "Is it safe though, to have us here? I would not wish to bring harm to your family or your home."

His anxiety was apparent in the lines of his face. Without thinking, Clara reached up to touch his cheek and he captured her hand in his.

"We'll set a watch. Meanwhile, you are all guests of the Whittingtons. They will not move against us here, not in the home of a family favoured by the Crown. We can rest while we formulate a plan to stop the Tradists."

Nessa cleared her throat, and Clara withdrew from the Captain's arms.

"You fought bravely today, Cat," he said, before narrowing his eyes. "Though I don't recall giving you leave to do battle."

The young pilot blushed, "Technically it was a rescue, not a battle."

The Captain let out a chuckle before grimacing. He held his side as he steadied his breath.

"Let's take a look, shall we?" said Himmat, as he pulled out his medical kit.

Mouse helped Clara pour the tea while Himmat and Ness checked the Captain's injuries.

"No permanent damage it appears. Your ribs may be bruised, but not broken. Do tell, what horrors compelled you to take on Corring and his men without aid?" Nessa asked, her biting tone softened by a smile.

"Oh, the usual," said the Captain Duke, accepting a cup of tea from Mouse with a grateful smile. "Defending ladies' honour. Holding degenerates to account for their sins."

"Naturally," Clara smirked.

Her mother's return—with sandwiches—put an end to the discussion. She sent their butler to help the Captain find a fresh shirt in Archie's room, and when he returned, Clara did her best not to notice how the borrowed shirt was just a touch too small in the shoulders, and the thin fabric stretched tight over his muscular form. As they ate, she told her mother of her brother's work at Lovelace and the exhibit at the Crystal Palace. The company kept to lighter subjects, and her mother never enquired further about the Captain's injuries or reason for their visit apart from mentioning there would be a hot bath drawn for his room.

Clara looked around the parlour at her crew. Mouse was animatedly telling the Captain of his lessons at Lovelace, Cat by his side. Nessa sat in amiable silence on the sofa opposite. Himmat had taken a plate of sandwiches with him, leaving to organize the rest of the pilots into watches for the night. It was a harmonious scene, one that made Clara's heart glad after so many months apart. The Captain Duke looked up and caught her eye, giving a roguish look that made her blush.

"A lovely young man this Olivier, is he not, Clara?" her

mother asked, sitting beside her.

"Why, yes. A mutual acquaintance introduced us in London. He's an explorer, you might say."

"Indeed," Mrs. Whittington replied, her innocent tone belying the glint of mischief in her eye. She pretended to stifle a yawn. "Well, I'm going up. Good night, everyone. I do hope you will make yourselves at home and all sleep comfortably tonight."

With a kiss to her daughter's forehead, Mrs. Whittington left the pilots to their own devices. They conversed about the various developments of the past number of weeks until the clock struck midnight, reminding them of the passing time. Clara led the way upstairs, happy to discover the fires lit and candles burning in the spare rooms of the east wing. Cat and Mouse claimed the Pearl Suite as their own. Nessa, the Blue Room.

When Clara and the Captain reached the door of the third room at the end of the passage, she fell silent. The Captain Duke was holding his arm close to his body, his chest rising and falling with slow, measured breaths. She wanted to say something, but while she had dreamed and wished for this moment—to see him, to have his steady presence at her side, to be in his arms again—the words to convey her feelings escaped her. Say something, she thought, as she willed herself to speak.

"It has a lovely view. Well, it is dark now, but in the morning you can see. I hope it is comfortable enough. I mean, there is the matter of your ribs and all, but you will tell us if you need anything at all," Clara babbled. "Good night, Captain."

The Captain stopped her as she moved to leave him,

placing a hand on her arm. She blushed, and cursed this sudden onslaught of timidity. With a deep breath, Clara summoned her courage. She raised her eyes to find him staring.

And smiling.

That smile.

"Clara," he whispered, taking her hand.

The Captain Duke cupped the back of her head and guided her mouth to his own. Clara curled her fingers into his shirt as she rose to her toes to deepen the kiss, relishing the sensation of his arm wrapping around her and pulling her close. Senseless to the world around them, they moved as one until the Captain's back was against the wood panelling. A sharp intake of breath, and Clara recalled his injury. But he only held her closer, burying his fingers in her hair as they poured all the things left unsaid between them into each other.

The months of close proximity. The terrible weeks of separation. Clara felt giddy and dizzy, in awe of the man who stood before her, a man whose path was so wonderfully entwined with her own. She wished she could gush to the whole world of his character, his quirks, his fierceness and bravery, his humour, his touch. She laughed softly, his lips brushing over hers. She could feel his smile.

"What is it?" he asked.

She looked up at him, seeing moonlight striking his fiery hair and christening his brow. Her lips parted to speak the words inaugurated in her heart.

Sudden footsteps alerted them they were not alone, and they broke apart a moment before the housekeeper turned the corner, fresh sheets in hand.

"Miss Clara!" she exclaimed, with a warm smile as she curtsied. "So wonderful to have you home again. I put extra candlesticks in your room for reading, just as you like."

"Thank you, Mrs. Hutchins. I was just saying good night to our guest."

Clara cleared her throat. She waited another beat, but the veteran housekeeper was immobile. The Captain let out a sigh, but smiled as he took her hand and raised it to his lips.

"Sweet dreams, Clara."

Clara could feel her cheeks burning as she met his eyes, "Good night, Milo."

His hold tightened as though he might draw her into another embrace, housekeeper or no, but then he grinned and let her fingers slip through his own. Clara felt his eyes on her as she walked down the hall to her own rooms. She could still feel his lips pressed against her own as she drifted to sleep.

Chapter 12: In which our hero helps to discover an opportune irregularity

The Captain Duke was sitting on a sunny bench in the garden, dead leaves littered at his feet. He held a hand to his side as he savoured the warmth on his face and the clear crisp air, drawing deep and steady breaths. It was important to breathe regularly with an injury such as this—despite the pain it inflicted. Those who constricted their breathing were most often felled by pneumonia and infection. Rest was also critical, though he wished he could join as he watched Nessa train with the children. It gladdened his heart to see them laughing as they ducked and thrust and parried.

Clara was a vision, deep in conversation with her mother as they walked through the lush gardens together. The resemblance was uncanny in both mannerism and appearance. Mrs. Whittington had taken the news of their profession in stride, though Clara had been sensible with the details she chose to share.

The crews had begun to gather in Newport, ship by ship. Peg brought news from Master Tims on her way south. Madge took the longest to arrive, making her way along the coastal tallports near London to ensure word of the Captain Duke sightings continued to spread. Each crew had taken up residence in a different inn along the Medina, to avoid suspicion. Tonight, the pirates and officers would be reunited at Whittington Manor, to dine and to discuss their next move against the Tradists.

The soft sweep of heavy skirts against the paving stones broke the Captain Duke from his reverie. He stood as Clara and her mother drew near.

"Mrs. Whittington, Miss Whittington," he said with a small bow.

Clara's mother graced them with a warm smile, "Your colour has improved greatly, Mr. Olivier. The country air is healing, is it not?"

"It is certainly an improvement over London," Clara replied, her eyes never leaving the Captain's. "How are you feeling today?"

"Much improved, thanks to the restorative powers of your beautiful home."

The Whittington women beamed at the compliment.

"You flatter us, Mr. Olivier, but I shall accept your praise," said Mrs. Whittington. "It brings me great pleasure to see our estate come back to life. Now, if you will be so kind to excuse me, I must check on the dinner preparations. Do call me when our dear pirates arrive."

With that, Mrs. Whittington left for the house, waving to the sword-wielding children as she passed. Clara shook her head as she joined him on the bench.

"And I thought I was the reckless one," she said, laughing softly. "My dear mother has embraced our cause most eagerly."

"Shockingly, I am not surprised at all," the Captain grinned.

"Captain!"

"Well, what did she say?"

"Only that she trusts me and my good judgement," Clara replied with an audacious wink.

They were alone again, a rare opportunity in the hustle and bustle of the last few days. But just as the Captain Duke parted his lips to speak—of the night of his kidnapping, of the rescue and that kiss, of the nature of his feelings for her and all he had dreamed about their future while in captivity—Nessa called to them from the training grounds.

The Captain turned his head to see her waving them over with a wide grin, Cat and Mouse at her side. With a sigh, he rose and helped Clara to her feet. But rather than releasing her hand, he met her eyes as he tucked it into the crook of his arm. The blush that rose to her cheeks matched his own colour he was sure. But he was too pleased to be bothered. And so they walked together along the garden path to meet their crew.

"Well, what have we here?" he asked.

"Our Cat has decided she would prefer to be part of the action next time," said Nessa. "Officially, that is."

With a grand sigh, the Captain Duke turned to Cat, who stood tall and proud with a cavalier smile.

"You know the rule, Cat. Not until you've bested Nessa in a duel."

"I am ready, Captain."

"Oh?" he replied.

"Oh?" repeated Nessa, arms akimbo.

"I agree," Clara said, lifting her chin—such a familiar

gesture, it brought a wide smile to the Captain Duke's face. "She's our best pilot, an expert strategist, a fine fighter and has been invaluable in our efforts to maintain our records and logbooks after the Haven burned. I support her pledge, as both friend and quartermaster."

Cat's expression shifted from that of one anxious to prove something, to the calm resolve of one who knows herself.

"Thank you, Quartermaster Clara," she said with a bow.

The Captain looked from one to the other, before meeting Nessa's eyes. She shrugged.

"Well, what will it be? Swords? Marksmanship? Hand to hand? Choose your field of battle."

Cat shook her head, "Gliders."

"Gliders?"

"Aye, I choose the sky. A race, if you will. If I can outfly you, you name me a full pilot and member of this crew."

"Do you agree to the terms, Ness?" the Captain asked.

Nessa laughed, a deep belly laugh.

"I do. Ready your equipment, I say sundown tonight before we enjoy the feast."

Cat shook Nessa's hand as well as the Captain's before running off to practice drills with her brother.

As the sun began its course to the edge of the horizon, the gliders raced over the tree tops toward the house. The crew was gathered in the garden, cheering and hollering as the pilots banked against the autumn breezes to circle the manor and come to a running stop on the garden path. Cat might have won by a full length, except she finished with her trademark flourish, somersaulting to a stop with her glider wings tucked in and pistols drawn, grinning ear to ear.

She won by half a length instead.

Mrs. Whittington, designated as impartial judge for the competition, announced her victory to a roar of applause as the pirates welcomed her. Nessa took her defeat with grace and congratulated her young charge, gifting her a small brooch with spread wings she had been saving for the occasion.

In their distraction, the group nearly missed the airship approaching their position as it broke through the cloud bank to the north. Madge was the first to notice the merchant vessel, growing larger by the minute as it diverted from the route to Newport—headed straight for Whittington Manor.

Swift as the breeze, the pirates paused their revelry to ready their defences. Mouse ushered Mrs. Whittington indoors while Peg and Himmat's crews rallied to the airship. Madge and Nessa organized their pilots along the terrace and gables—but as soon as Nessa reached the roof with Cat and the rest of the glider crew, she signalled to Clara and the Captain. She cupped her hand to her mouth as she shouted to them:

"Hold off, it's the *Ariadne*!"

They held their positions until the airship was close enough for them to see Trick waving from the bow, Captain Buchanan at his side. They docked above the garden, next to the Captain's airship. A small platform elevator was lowered from the underside of the vessel. To the pirates' surprise, Archie was among the first to descend, and beside him… Professor Georgina Jameson Sewell.

The pilots looked to Clara and the Captain for direction as Archie helped the Professor down from the platform, which hovered a few feet from the ground. He was smiling ear to ear as he led her to join the others, tucking her hand in the crook of his arm. She looked decidedly nervous.

"Archie, welcome home," Clara addressed her brother with a tight smile. "We were not expecting company."

"I can explain," he replied, looking to his companion. "We can explain everything."

The Captain Duke raised an eyebrow at that, but nodded his assent to Clara. His attention was soon diverted. Captain Buchanan and Trick were the next to descend.

"Hello, old friend," the Captain Duke called. "You look well."

Trick's eyes were filled with emotion, but he pressed his lips together and gave a simple nod. The Captain crossed the lawn to embrace his first mate, before drawing apart with a sharp intake of breath.

"Aye, serves you right, Captain, getting yourself kidnapped," Trick scowled. "What the devil were ye thinking?"

But the Captain Duke could not help the smile that followed. He was more than happy to receive a dressing down if it meant Trick was back to feeling like himself.

Nessa arrived to stand with them, holstering her

weapons and smoothing the wisps of blonde hair that had escaped her plait during the race. But her eyes were all for Marie.

"Glad to see you are well, Olivier," said Captain Buchanan, as she approached.

"I believe I owe that in part to you, Captain," he said with a small bow. "You have my thanks."

The famed pilot showed her pleasure at his deference, but quickly resumed her business-like expression.

"I see we have interrupted your celebration. We would have sent word, but we did not trust the wireless after the Professor cautioned against its use."

"Oh?" Clara responded, her eyes narrowing.

"I'll let the Professor explain," said Captain Buchanan.

The Captain Duke traded a wordless look with Clara, questions filling both of their eyes.

"We can use my ship," he replied.

The Captain's cabin was filled with their closest allies…and one whose allegiance was yet unknown. Trick, Nessa, Marie and Cat took up position on one side of the room, with Archie and the Professor on the other. Mouse soon joined their party as well, looking between his sister and Archie before taking a seat on the bench beside his mentor.

When they were all seated, Nessa cleared her throat loudly. Realizing all eyes were on her, the Professor blushed and stood to address the group.

"Thank you, all of you, for the opportunity to explain my actions. I understand now that I may have…erred in placing my trust in certain individuals, but I swear to you I will not stop until I can redress the wrongs committed in my name."

"Why don't we begin with how you came to this revelation?" asked Clara.

Professor Sewell looked to Archie for reassurance, drew a deep breath, and began.

"I was approached by Admiral Flint some time ago—at a benefit for disabled veterans. He was rather interested in my early work on automation and offered a partnership to further my research. I did not realize the nature of their intentions to use my creations for ill. I was blinded by the science—it was not until Archie raised his concerns that my perspective shifted. I did not believe him—at first. But I took those concerns to the Admiral while we were in London for the showcase, and his response was… unsatisfactory, to say the least. Then the cretin had the temerity to ask for my hand. And he did not take kindly to rejection. If it wasn't for Archie…"

Here, the Professor paused to take his hand—Clara had not noticed the bandage before.

"Archie! What happened?"

Her brother fidgeted, the colour rising on his neck. "Ah, well, there may have been an exchange of words, and you see, I've been practicing my sparring with Trick and Mouse—to promote his recovery, as physical therapy for his arm—and when the Admiral became aggressive I—I may have struck him on the nose."

Captain Buchanan let out a snort of laughter, "Do not

undersell your achievement. I heard you knocked him clear off his feet and broke his nose."

The room was silent as they all registered their shock—none quite so surprised as Clara.

"And what happened then?" she asked, incredulous.

"Well, we packed our research and left the Crystal Palace immediately," Professor Sewell continued. "Archie knew exactly where to go after Mrs. Branson-Honeycutt conveyed your message, and with Trick's assurances, Captain Buchanan eventually agreed to bring us to you."

"And you trust her change of heart?" the Captain Duke asked Marie, his eyes hard.

Captain Buchanan lifted her chin, "I do. I had my crew verify her tale. Admiral Flint has been misrepresenting himself and the interests of his allies to Professor Sewell, taking advantage of her desire to promote the interests of Lovelace University."

The Captain Duke nodded, "I am satisfied. Quartermaster?"

Clara was frowning, her brow knit into a puzzled crease as she considered the Professor's words. "You told my brother of the funds the Admiral was giving to your research. I have seen your factories, the work you produce. Your resources are already quite substantial. Why did you need his help?"

The Professor took a deep breath and sighed, "In all honesty, much of my inheritance has gone to the university. We have an excellent reputation, yet still there is a shocking unwillingness to fund our scholars. I funded some of the research chairs myself. The patents of my work are profitable, yes, but in practice we rarely recoup the cost of the labour from those we help. There are those like me, except whose families do not have the privileges of mine to encourage their recovery. Their mechanicals must be individually fitted anew as the youngest grow, and each year we discover better methods to make them comfortable and adaptable to their needs. In short, I wanted more resources. This partnership would have given me the means to provide these services to those in need, gratis. But the cost is too great."

Cat leapt down from her perch on a windowsill, "Wait one moment. How was the Admiral going to afford this endeavour? Where did he get the resources?"

"I assumed it would be a joint enterprise. There were a number of merchants on the council," the Professor replied. "The Admiral was merely its chairperson."

"I think he's been using you as an excuse for greater resources from the Crown," Captain Buchanan interjected, pulling a letter from a hidden pocket in her artfully tailored jacket. "I remain a member in good standing of the Association of Merchant Traders. After speaking with Ness and listening to your concerns, I found an interesting detail in my copy of their latest periodical report that I think you ought to see."

She passed the report to the Captain Duke, who examined its contents. He let out a bitter laugh as he discovered her meaning.

"Well, we are caught," he said, passing the letter to Clara. "They actually have a line in their accounting for their losses to pirating."

But Clara's frown only deepened as she scanned the

paper, gesturing to Cat to join her. The two conferred quietly before Cat fled the room.

"What is it?" asked the Captain Duke.

"This is a substantial sum," Clara replied. "But we have been keeping careful track of our figures, particularly after Robbie's betrayal and our change in strategy."

Within minutes, Cat returned with an armful of receipt books. Trick and Mouse helped to clear a table, and all gathered around Clara as she checked the sums.

"According to our tabulations—even with the increases we have seen in bounty over years past—a generous accounting would make up for barely a quarter of the value of the goods they claim were diverted."

"Well, we are not the only pirates in the Empire," said the Captain Duke.

"No, but you are the largest group—and the luckiest I might add," said Captain Buchanan.

"Extraordinary," Clara said, shaking her head.

"How do you mean?" asked Nessa.

"The faction of Tradists led by the Admiral. They must have diverted the resources themselves, and blamed the likes of the Captain Duke," Clara exclaimed as she turned to him. "They have played upon your own myth to justify their excesses and fraud."

The Captain was stunned.

"They stole from themselves," he whispered, shaking his head. "They stole from themselves and passed the cost of their deception onto shopkeepers like Tims."

"Of course," added Trick. "They would not even need to pay the Crown's taxes on goods they claimed were stolen. They have been reaping the profits and shortchanging the shops, pretending scarcity."

"I wondered at that," added Captain Buchanan. "Something did not add up in their accounts of the conditions they encountered in transport. My crews and I have travelled the world, and never have we seen losses on this scale."

The Captain began to pace the room, anger in every step. "The scale of this…our efforts to help those in need used to further their subjugation. It has all been for naught! Everything—every battle, every raid, every sack of grain—has been stolen back tenfold by those who need it least. They have starved us all."

His anguished outpouring was interrupted by a soft snicker. Clara had the smile of a cat in a creamery.

"How can you laugh?" he asked, incredulous.

"Don't you see?" Clara asked, her mirth increasing as she looked around. "We've caught them. With a ledger!"

Her explanation was met with a matching chuckle from Captain Buchanan.

"It is true. I doubt they expected to encounter pirates with such detailed recordkeeping and modern accounting practices, yet here we are. Goodness, you even have receipts, signed by the Tradists themselves."

The Captain Duke stared in wonder at the pile before them. Clara had incorporated the receipt books into her scheme from the start, a means of convincing targets of their legitimacy as 'inspectors' to collect the tithes without resorting to violence. He picked one up and flipped through. Signatures on every page verifying the value and nature of all the goods they had appropriated since late summer.

He turned to Clara, whose shocked expression matched his own.

"Brilliant. Clara, you are brilliant!"

He swept her into his arms and spun in a circle, eliciting a sparkling laughter from her lips. Lips that captured his own as she tilted his face towards her, in full view of the crew. It was but a second, but the Captain Duke felt as though the axis of the world had paused for this moment of unadulterated joy as he held her in his arms.

"There is more," said Cat, excitement in her voice.

Mouse piped in. "We think we know where they are keeping it."

"Keeping what?" the Captain asked.

"The loot!" they said in unison.

Every face turned to them.

"What? How?"

"When we followed the Admiral after the dinner party, they didn't fly straight to Newport. They went all the way to the western end of the Isle first before turning back. We followed until he disappeared into a ravine. I could not get close enough to see exactly where."

"There are smugglers' caves along the coast," said Clara. "Could they have hidden their plunder?"

The Captain Duke grinned, "Quartermaster, gather the crew. Tonight, we hunt for treasure."

Chapter 13: In which our heroine needles her enemies

The waves broke against the sharp rocks jutting upwards from the water like broken teeth. The odd geography of the coast was known as the Needles, a chalky outcropping of sea stacks reaching away from the island and its pebbled beaches and towering cliffs. Clara felt her heart turn over at the sight of the small glider as it skimmed the waves, flying low and fast as Cat navigated the coastal winds.

Too fast. She's flying too fast, Clara fretted.

One misjudged shift in weight and she'd be slammed into cliffs or taken by punishing waves. But just as Clara tensed to rise from her lookout spot to shout a warning, Cat threaded her glider sideways through a gap in the rocks and banked towards the shore on the other side. She landed on the rocky beach, panting heavily.

"All clear. There's no one guarding the chine. Mouse is certain it's the one." she said between breaths, her excitement contagious.

With a wide smile, Clara signalled the airship hovering low over the waves, hidden from sight by the high western cliffs of the Isle of Wight. The Captain Duke gave the sharp rocks a wide berth as he steered the craft to the beach on the northern coast. Cat and Clara glided down together, landing near the mouth of a stream that trickled out from one of the island's many chines.

The shallow tributary bubbled over smooth stones beside lush green banks before disappearing into the ravine, carved by years of erosion. The pirates had to walk single file, the Captain and Clara leading the way. Halfway up the cliffs their progress was halted by a steeper fall, where the calm river tumbled over fallen rocks into a small pond before continuing its course to the sea.

"Ahoy, Captain!"

Mouse popped out from amidst a rockfall, startling Clara. The Captain halted his step for hairsbreadth before laughing. The boy was nearly jumping with excitement.

"What happened to 'quiet as a mouse?'" he teased. "Well, did you find our cave of wonders?"

"It's over here!"

Mouse led them to a moss-covered rock that looked as though it had not been disturbed in centuries—except the slab beneath it was worn smooth. The Captain Duke ran his hand along the crevice until he found a hold, and with a strong push the boulder slipped from its mooring, revealing a darkened passage concealed behind.

Clara called for tapers to be lit. She had to bend nearly in half to enter the cliffside, following Mouse as he disappeared around a sharp corner, but after a few paces the corridor gave way to a more comfortable cavern. This section had been carved deeper by human hands, with wooden planks to even out the roughness of the floor and protect against the damp. The light of their tapers did not reach the furthest corners, but it was enough. Clara and Mouse stared at their surroundings in wonder before calling for the Captain Duke to join them.

There were no chests spilling over with strange silver coins and strands of pearls. No precious objects looted from stormwrecks, or trove of priceless artifacts of times gone by. Only neat stacks of cast iron strongboxes, each half as wide as they were long with large handles on each end. There were dozens of them, stacked eight high where the ceiling allowed. Each was marked with the same symbol they had seen pinned to the Admiral's lapel and sealed with a gleaming Chubb lock.

The Captain gave a low whistle as he joined them, "This is no private stash. This must be the entire Tradist treasury."

A more thorough search of the cave produced a narrow flatbed trolley they used to carry three of the boxes back to the entrance of the hollow.

The pirates cheered their return with the bounty—then held their breath as Madge stepped forward. Chubbs were notorious for their difficulty, and she was the best lockpicker on the crew. For a quarter of an hour, they stood in silence as she bent to her task on the first of the boxes. And they groaned in unison as she tripped the regulator and the lock jammed.

The second one jammed within five minutes.

Madge swore loudly and stood, shaking her head, "I'm sorry, Captain. These new six-lever locks—I need better tools than I have with me here."

"Do we take them now and tip off the Tradists? Or should we wait and watch and try to steal the keys?" Clara mused. "It could be a trap."

The Captain Duke was frowning, "It's all or none. If

even one goes missing, they'll know they have been compromised."

"Can I try?" Mouse piped. "I read about these in my physics book."

Clara and the Captain traded a look. Madge shrugged and handed over her tools. The young boy sat with his tongue between his teeth as he carefully manipulated the levers. The only sound was that of the water flowing over the rocks as Mouse toiled, his movements slow and precise. Then a deep, satisfying click as the lock opened.

The shock on Mouse's face was matched by the Captain's. He opened the catch and lifted the heavy lid to reveal the gleaming bars within. Eyes wide as saucers, he stood back to let the rest of the crew see their bounty.

Clara and the Captain Duke stared at each other in wonder.

"How much can we carry?" she asked, tilting her head as she tried to calculate the weight and number of the chests. "We only brought one ship."

"All of it," he replied. "We'll do more runs if needed." Then he turned to the assembled pirates. "Well? What are you waiting for? Cat, you're our recordkeeper. Log every chest as best you can. Trick, take the airship up to the cliffs and lower the loading deck—oh, and lose the ballast, won't be needing that now. Everyone else, pair up and move quick. I want this ship loaded by the noon hour."

The crew snapped to attention, all grinning ear to ear as they relieved the cavern of its contents. Clara climbed to the clifftop overlooking the chine, taking in the view of the coastline as she breathed the sea-scented air. She wanted to hold onto this moment, with the waves crashing against the shore and victory on the horizon. The Captain soon joined her, wearing a thoughtful expression as they stood side by side, watching the pirates work.

"There's a storeroom near the Haven we can use while Madge and her team break the rest of the locks. We'll need to send Himmat and his crew to get more of our ships in Newport. Once we've loaded everything, we'll do a straight run to Keswick and return by tomorrow eve."

"Nessa and I should be back by then as well," Clara replied with a nod. "I secured an audience for the morning."

She brushed her fingers against the back of the Captain's hand. He reached for her, wrapping an arm around her waist as he kissed her before leaning his forehead against hers.

"Clara, my lucky star," he whispered. "Be a dear and do not tarry. We must celebrate our victory."

She smiled, "Aye, Captain."

Chapter 14: In which our heroine seeks a favour from an old friend

Clara stood at the bow of the *Ariadne*, watching the Isle of Wight fade into the horizon as she crossed to the mainland.

But this time she was not running away.

Nessa joined her, resting her elbows on the railing as they looked over the landscape below.

"How does it feel?" she asked, turning to Clara with a smile.

"Different from the last time. But I am different since the last time," Clara replied.

"Change is good. Many things will change after this, I'm sure. We'll all be rich as Midas."

"What will you do with your part of it?"

"That depends. If the Captain has need of me, I'll be there."

"Which captain?" Clara teased.

Nessa gave her a playful shove, but her eyes wandered to the prow of the ship where Captain Buchanan stood, conferring with her pilots. "I may do some travelling this storm season. The thought had crossed my mind."

Catching their stare, Captain Buchanan joined their party. She wore a tailored jacket and long skirts, a Windsor knot at her throat.

"We'll reach our destination in a few hours. I would suggest we use this time to review our petition once more. It is not every day one has an audience with royalty."

They waited in the antechamber to be announced. The apartments were luxurious and bright, and filled with an atmosphere of joy from the safe delivery of the Princess' firstborn. Princess Beatrice had birthed a son, and she remained at Windsor as she recovered, her husband never leaving her side. They were not receiving official visitors—but a childhood friend was a different matter.

The lady in waiting opened the doors and stood aside, her hands folded precisely.

"Your highness, may I present Lady Clara Whittington, Professor Georgina Jameson Sewell and Captain Marie Buchanan."

They entered and curtsied. Princess Beatrice wore her dressing gown, seated in a chair beside an ornate bassinet. She had the glow of a new mother, enchanted by her tiny son.

"Clara, he's an absolute dear. You must come look."

With a smile, Clara crossed the room to sit beside her. The child slept soundly, swaddled in fine cloth.

"You are feeling well?" Clara asked, after cooing over

the child and making all the appropriate affirmations to his health and comeliness.

“It was not so terrible as they say. I would not have minded if the home secretary had made himself scarce for the occasion, but Henry and mother were by my side. She was quite happy. Though she insists that she shall call me ‘Baby’ still,” the Princess replied with a laugh before growing serious. “Now, my dear Clara, I insist that you tell me why you are really here.”

Clara traded a look with Captain Buchanan and the Professor, before turning back to Princess Beatrice.

“We need your help.”

Chapter 15: In which our heroine engineers a most favourable outcome

The manor glowed with the gaiety within as the long gallery was transformed into a pirate's mess for the occasion. Extra candles were brought out as they celebrated their bounty—and the triumphant return of Clara with royal letters of pardon for every member of the crew. News of Admiral Flint's arrest for treason against the Crown was the cherry on top.

Crews toasted one another, telling tales of how they planned to enjoy their share of the bounty. Trick spoke of opening a music school—word of his performance at the Crystal Palace had spread with critical acclaim in the press. Cat planned to keep her portion for the purchase of her own airship one day. Mouse, when pressed, admitted that he wanted to further his studies. Archie and the Professor agreed to tutor him—he could afford the best schools once he passed the general examinations. The others spoke of restoring the Haven to its former glory, of new ships and fine clothes. Mrs. Cottingham was certain to have a well-stocked larder with all the business coming her way.

Clara caught the Captain Duke's eye and they slipped outside to take in the cool air.

"Tell me again," the Captain demanded, leaning against the balcony railing as he uncorked a bottle of champagne. "What she said when you showed her your receipt books."

Clara laughed, extending her glass to be filled. "She said she was not the first Queen to make allies of pirates—and doubted she would be the last."

"And then?"

"And then she sent for the home secretary and dismissed us. But not before informing Marie that she required a new Minister of Trade and expected her letters of reference to be delivered within a fortnight."

"The Tradists have lost their leader, our allies are ascendant, and you, Miss Whittington, have enriched us all with your cleverness."

The Captain Duke set the bottle on the rail and pulled her into his arms to dance about the balcony, twirling her in the starlight as she laughed. When they reached the far west edge, they stopped to take in the view of the Captain's airship nestled in the garden.

"We'll need to build a tallport," she said. "Just a small one. A single tier—perhaps two."

"Are you so determined to turn your family home into a haven?" he asked.

"Only while we are rebuilding," she replied. "I wouldn't dream of relocating our crew."

The Captain was silent as he stared into the distance, but he pulled her hand to his lips.

"Captain?" she whispered, before biting her lip. "Milo. You have not said what you will do with your share of the treasure. Do not assume it has escaped my attention."

He laughed, "I would never make such a presumption.

Your powers of observation are now legendary."

Clara laughed, and pulled the tie from his hair to set the fiery mane loose around his shoulders. It fell like a curtain around her as he ducked his head to kiss her. Then he grew serious.

"Clara, we have changed everything. Perhaps this new world will not need pirates such as I."

"What do you mean?"

"We have the ear of the Queen. The rogue Tradists have no leadership and will be forced to account for their actions against the common people. We won," he said, stroking her hair. "I never intended to be a pirate forever. I only wished to see a little more fairness in this world."

"My Robin Hood," she said, with a teasing smile.

He chuckled and looked down.

"What is it?" she asked.

"You promise not to tell?"

"Your secret is safe with me," she replied, her curiosity piqued.

The Captain Duke directed her gaze to the airship.

"*The Golden Arrow.*"

"The—your airship? *The Golden Arrow*? Is that its name?"

"Based on an old ballad from childhood. I loved the audacity of those tales of Robin Hood and his band of Merry Men. I dreamed of being a hero, like him."

"And what do you dream of now?"

"You," the Captain replied. "I dream of you. And what do you dream of?"

Clara's heart turned over, "Adventure. I want to see the world. I have tasted but a sliver of this life and I want more. But I cannot imagine that life without you by my side."

"Then, as we finish our task of dismantling the Tradists once and for all, I shall endeavour to make your every dream come true."

The Captain Duke kissed her under the stars, pledging himself to her with his lips, pressing his body against hers.

"Then come with me," she whispered. "We'll fly together."

The two pirates stole through the hallways and away from the revelry. They fled the manor through the garden, toward their airship, hand in hand.

Chapter 16: In which our heroine holds her ground and embraces the winds of change

The knock on the door was abrupt.

Sunlight poured through the cabin windows onto tangled sheets. The Captain Duke traced the curve of Clara's cheek as her eyes fluttered open.

The knocking was insistent.

The Captain ignored the muffled voices beyond the door and snuggled further beneath the linens with Clara in his arms. Her brown curls were loose over her bare shoulders. He pulled the blanket over their heads to better ignore the rest of the world. She gave a sleepy, satisfied smile as he placed a finger to her lips.

"Captain? Clara? You had better dress yourselves. We have company."

"Trick. Not now," he yelled.

"Clara!"

This time it was Nessa hollering.

"Your ex has arrived, and he brought friends."

With that, Clara was wide awake. Planting a kiss on the Captain's forehead, she leapt from the bed to dress. Slim black pants, a loose linen shirt, her favourite purple overskirt and a wide black belt. The Captain begrudgingly left the bed to find his own trousers before helping her to buckle her pistols about her waist.

"Clara, my shirt?"

"On the deck, I believe."

"Ah, well. This will do," he said, pulling his long blue coat from the hook.

Clara raised an eyebrow, pausing before she opened the door. He crossed to her and wrapped his arms around her waist from behind.

"Ready?" he whispered in her ear.

Her response was a roguish grin as she opened the door of the cabin and stormed out. The Captain followed, nodding to Trick who held out his shirt with his hook. Clara and Nessa were already halfway down the ropes, so he threw it into the cabin before following.

The pirates were assembled in front of the manor, armed to the teeth. They faced a paltry crew of young men in fine jackets, led by Alexander Corring.

"What is the meaning of this?" demanded Clara as she reached the front.

The Captain Duke stood behind her, enjoying the look of apoplectic fury Corring directed to him. Then Corring smoothed his jacket and addressed Clara.

"I warned you there would be consequences," he said. "Admiral Flint chose to remain within the confines of politeness, but I am in charge now. I will give you but one chance to give up your unlawful endeavours. Return our property and submit to my protection, or we will be forced to take drastic measures."

"Like hell I will," Clara replied.

There was a soft thud as the glove hit the ground—at her brother's feet.

Clara's breath caught.

She had fled the Isle of Wight to avoid this very circumstance, of her brother being pressed to defend her honour by the knave who stood, red-faced and smug, at the door of her family's home. Then her eyes narrowed as her fear crystallized into a deep and burning rage.

How dare he.

Without a second thought, she stooped to pick up the offending garment.

Alexander's mouth gaped in astonishment, to her extreme satisfaction.

"I accept your challenge. I choose pistols. Name the field—or would you prefer to settle this now?"

"You cannot!"

"Says who?"

"Clara, don't be ridiculous. Archie, be a man and tell her."

Her brother traded a look with the Captain before turning to Corring.

"I think Clara is quite capable of expressing herself on this matter," he said.

"I am happy to offer my services as a second, should you require them," the Captain Duke said, taking a step forward to stand at her side.

Corring seethed, looking between them. Then he appeared to remember the men gathered behind him.

"If the gentlemen present will not accept my challenge, an apology will suffice. I wish no violence against a lady."

Clara rolled her eyes. That was quite enough posturing. She wanted an end to this business, once and for all. She pulled her father's duelling pistols from the twin holsters at her hips, polished to a gleam. She spun them on her fingers and cocked them as she walked forward, her skirt swishing behind her.

The first bullet hit the ground to the right of his feet, and he danced away from her.

"Christ, woman! Are you mad?"

"I am done with you, Alexander," she said, firing a second shot to his left. "I am done with your threats to me and my family. I am done with your scheming and your whingeing. I am done with politely explaining our incompatibilities."

Corring stumbled as she continued her progress down the lane towards them, his men hurrying backwards in full retreat.

"I am Clara Whittington, and I will defend my own honour," she called as she pursued them down the lane. "Land or sky—you'd best not cross me or mine."

As her former fiancé turned tail and ran, overtaking his men as they fled the property, Clara smiled to herself. She holstered her pistols and turned to the pirates assembled in front of her home.

Nessa was beaming, Captain Buchanan at her side, nodding in approval. Cat and Mouse stood with Trick, weapons at the ready to join her if needed. Professor Sewell and her mother were hand in hand behind Archie, watching the scene with white faces, but her mother raised a hand to her heart with a smile of reassurance. Peg and Madge and Himmat and all the crew were grinning as they looked to her. And the Captain Duke…

"A cheer, for our Quartermaster!" he called.

The breeze carried their words far and wide as they shouted together:

To the winds, to the clouds, to a life lived well,
Take me up to the sky!
To the heavens above and the land far below,
Pilot, keep to the sky!
To the sun on your face and the stars in your eyes,
Clara! Give us the sky!

Epilogue

The girls were nearly identical, only those closest to them could tell them apart. One lay sideways in a high-backed chair, dangling her stocking-clad feet over the arm. The other rested in the window seat, her knees drawn up to her chin as she observed the world beyond the manor with thoughtful, hazel eyes. The afternoon lull made their eyelids heavy, but they fought against the lure of sleep.

A rustle of skirts as the young girl in the window stood on the sill, pressing her nose to the glass. Her sister propped herself on her elbows.

"Do you see it?"

"Maybe. Pass me my telescope."

The girl in the chair slid off and picked up the toy, handing it up to her sister while she pulled a matching one from the pocket fastened about her waist in a neat bow. They scanned the horizon together.

"I see her!"

"You do not, that's a cloud. We have to be certain this time. No false alarms."

"No, over there! Look to the east."

They strained to make out the tiny speck through the

glass, but soon the familiar shape was unmistakable. The girls looked to each other, breaking into matching smiles and dashing from the room.

They bolted for the stairs and slid backwards down the railing to reach the foyer, landing on a heavy indigo and cream pillow placed there as a concession to their welfare.

They paused at the door to slip on their shoes, discarded in a haphazard pile. After a moment's confusion, as one ended up with two left feet and the other with two right shoes, they made the switch and raced out the door.

Their father was already in the garden, shading his eyes from the afternoon sun as he looked to the east. His hair—the same shade as the girls' fiery curls—was tied neatly back, though the wind blew wisps free of the binding as he turned to them with a broad smile.

"Ah, my little lookouts!"

One of the twins leapt into his arms as her sister took him by the sleeve. For many nights he had sent them to sleep with stories of their beloved mother, hoping for her safe return. They walked together to the tallport on the hill.

The airship was painted a deep blue. Blue as the coat of the man who now tracked its course through the skies. Its hull had seen a thousand aliases, but it now bore its true name in a looping scroll: *The Golden Arrow*. A dark-haired woman waved to the three figures below, racing to join them the moment the airship docked.

Clara was home from another adventure, with many more tales to tell.

The adventure doesn't end here!

Become a patron for access to bonus chapters, character profiles and exclusive previews of what I'm working on next…

patreon.com/RebeccaDiem

Author's Note

When I first crafted the setting of the Tales of the Captain Duke, I knew I wanted to create a steampunk version of Victorian England. I grew up playing in the den of my grandparents' house, under the watchful eye of a large portrait of Queen Victoria herself. My natural curiosity and Canadian upbringing led me to research the lives and stories of British royalty—but I always wondered at the stories of the people around them. What were their hopes, desires, dreams and fears?

There are so many gems in our histories. So many tales to tell of those who came before us who would help to shape the world. Many of the brightest stars we know by name—Ada Lovelace, Marie Curie, Florence Nightingale, even Hypatia. But there are so many more who fill our skies!

When I was crafting the dinner party scene, I wanted to hint at some of those stories. Dorota, in the story, pays tribute to Bronislawa Sklodowska—more commonly known as the elder sister of Marie Curie. It was Bronislawa who insisted on her sister's education after the death of their mother, who began studying at a secret Polish university that permitted women students, and who led the way to the Sorbonne in France where Marie would follow. And Khadijah's inspiration is Huda Sha'rawi, the pioneering Egyptian feminist scholar, who insisted on furthering her education and played a leading role in the nationalist movement of her country, even founding the Egyptian

Feminist Union and challenging the social codes of her time. Her memoir about her early life helped the western world to better understand the experience of an upper middle-class Arab woman.

These women lived and studied during the Victorian era, and I would like to think that they would be very pleased with the many women who pursue higher education, study medicine and continue to fight for social justice today.

One of my favourite elements to play with in the steampunk genre is the social and cultural impacts of these technological breakthroughs. In the universe of the Tales of the Captain Duke, I wanted to tell the story of how those innovations influence the lives of the characters in different ways. Clara, the debutante turned 'liberator', chooses to use her privilege and education to benefit others. Nessa, a woman of the working class, is able to significantly expand her employment options. And little Cat is growing up with the knowledge that she is equally capable to her peers, with mentors who support and encourage her at every opportunity.

I hope that you have enjoyed these tales. There are many more stories lurking between the pages—ones that I hope one day to tell. In the meantime, I encourage you to seek out those stories in the margins of history, and to lend your voice to bringing them into the light.

Rebecca Diem
April 2018

Acknowledgements

Five years ago I was sitting in a café, playing with a story idea about a girl who ran away… and the tale definitely grew in the telling.

This quartet of novellas, my very first series, is finally finished. But I could not have done it without my crew.

Thank you once again to Sarah Dier-McComb for the breathtaking artwork. I am so honoured to have your paintings front and centre, and I brag about your many talents to any who will listen, as any big sister would.

Thank you, Arden Dier, my first editor and beta reader, for being there from the first draft to the last. Your advice and insight took these stories to another level.

Thank you to Steve Armstrong, for crafting the perfect covers and finding every iteration of porthole for me to choose from. Seeing the quartet together, at last—I have no words for the joy your work brings to my heart.

Many thanks to my beta readers, Pattie Miller and Lori Steuart, who are responsible for Clara's mother making her debut. Thank you for your vote of confidence, and for your enthusiasm at a time that I needed it most.

Thank you to Kieran Flanagan for grabbing coffee with a stranger and sharing your stories of the Isle of Wight. You helped to bring this tale home.

Thank you to Todd Clark and the Toronto Steampunk Society for welcoming into your ranks. You gave me a place at your table, and you will always have a place at mine.

Thank you to the fine folks of Capital Espresso, Dark Horse, Early Bird, and my beloved Bean Cellar.

Thank you to Mrs. Penny McKay for instilling an early love of reading and pressing new books into my hands at every opportunity. Thank you to Catherine Miller for helping me to believe I could write one myself.

Thank you to Alice, Ashley, Danny, Lori, Donna, Nerissa, Priscilla, Andrada, Bryan, Letitia, Amanda, and Alex for your help at the conventions and getting my books where they need to go.

Thank you to Diana, Emily, Laura, Val, Erin, Jackie, Nina, Ruth, Caitlynn, Jack, Pam, Jon, Paola, Guru, Steph, Rogue, Tom, Dominik, Dave and Twiggy for, among other things, inspiration, consolation, ascendency and delight. You wonderful humans make my life brighter.

Thank you, Kyle. Our adventure is just beginning.

And finally, thank you to my family. My parents, Ray and Kelly; my siblings, Andrew, Sarah K., Sarah P., and Leah (and Daisy, Gryffindor and Lily!); my grandparents, Ron and Marilyn, Bob and Peggie; and my extended fam of aunts, uncles and cousins. You have been my greatest cheerleaders from that first book launch. I wouldn't be here without you at my side. I love you all more than words.

Rebecca Diem
April 2018

PATREON | REBECCA DIEM

A very special thank you to my earliest supporters on Patreon!
Thank you all for believing in me. ❤

Kelly & Ray McComb
Gary Hilson
Adrienne Romani
Mallory Donaldson
Laura Sinclair
Grace Currie
Nina Nesseth
Andrew Dier-McComb
Heather Stoneman
Jackie Miller
Valorie Curry
Donna Lyons
Laura Rashotte

Ron & Marilyn McComb
Heather Stoneman
Spencer Turbitt
Ruth Gebremedhin
Aly Boltman
Lori Steuart
Andrew Stewart
Mathieu Perron
Wendy Browne
Alice Quinn
Rolando Henry
Kerry Chabot
Derek Breedon

Photo by Caitlynn Fairbarns

Rebecca Diem is a writer, music lover and nerd. She loves the steampunk genre for its ability to disrupt and re-imagine both history and the future.

An avid bookworm, Rebecca was honoured to receive a 'Nose in a Book' award from her elementary school librarian. Somewhere between reading Virginia Woolf and Neil Gaiman she began to write her own stories.

Rebecca now calls Toronto home and is on a never-ending quest to find the perfect café and writing spot.

Web: rebeccadiem.com
Email: rebeccadiemauthor@gmail.com
Facebook: RebeccaDiemAuthor
Twitter/Instagram: @kthnxbex
Patreon: patreon.com/RebeccaDiem

Thank you so much for supporting my work.
Please share, rate and review!

94648650R00078

Made in the USA
Columbia, SC
04 May 2018